DEMONHOST IRIS OF GAMMA

Part One: Fugitive

Rose Capybara

Kindle Direct Publishing

CONTENTS

PART ONE: FUGITIVE

CHAPTER 1: SLAUGHTERHOUSE

What Iris saw was a scene out of her worst nightmares, an abandoned storefront caked in blood and viscera. Robed figures lay scattered across her vision, all of them horrifically mutilated. Some had expressions of sheer terror, others spent their final moments attempting to hold their lacerated stomachs in. One which was unlucky enough to survive reached up at her, his mutilated entrails dispersed behind him. As though begging for a salvation which would never come, even if she were the ally the figure mistook her for.

Horrified, Iris unsuccessfully fought back the urge to vomit, adding her own bile to the puddles of blood and mucus soaking the concrete floor. She fell to her knees, snot streaming down her face as she took in the carnage before her. Her jeans and gloves were stained red by the cultist's lost blood, perhaps their final mark upon the world. The one reaching out to her finally collapsed, joining their comrades in death. In the back of her mind, Iris realized she was in great danger. The slaughter was very recent, meaning, its cause was near.

She jumped to her feet and saw it. The person she least wanted to see in this horrific structure, or rather, a grotesque mockery of his corpse. It was made up of thousands of writhing cylinders of flesh making up a crude humanoid figure. On all fours, its head buried into a cultist's entrails, it suddenly noticed and lurched towards her, scuttling forward.

Her own father.

Iris ran, but just as with the scattered corpses, she never had a hope of escape. It was simply too unnaturally rapid, pouncing on her back and pinning down all four of her limbs. The only mercy this bizarre monstrosity granted her was restraining her face-down so that she stared at scattered organs and blood rather than her father's gibbering face, splitting apart and reconstituting itself with fleshworms every time it emitted noise.

"You."

Shuttering, grinding, an approximation of speech by something which found it an unnatural action.

"Human. You are not like the others. You have... potential. You have goals, beyond a foolish desire for personal power. These utter morons met their end seeking to control something far beyond their feeble understanding. You arrived seeking something different entirely. You will have my aid."

His aid? This thing was the one that killed her father! Past the revulsion and horror dominating her continence, a flash of anger flared forth. Iris began sputtering, but her only reply was a sharp pain to the back of her neck. Then her consciousness blinked out.

Several minutes later, Iris found herself forced awake by burning pain throughout her body. It was a strange agony, lines deep within her forming a blazing inferno tracing their way, from deep within her chest to hear head to all four of her limbs. Her tears, previously shed in horror and despair, now flowed forth in anguish. Crawling to a wall, she leaned against it, surveying the room once more.

Iris' father was dead. She walked into a slaughterhouse and was assaulted by that grotesque creature in the shape of his body. She was surrounded by around two dozen more torn apart corpses, with the creature nowhere to be seen. Her jeans and jacket were utterly soaked in their blood. What was she going to do?

"Listen to me."

That voice again, grating, unnatural. She jerked her head around, looking for the source.

"What is your name?"

Finding nothing, Iris thought it must have been an auditory hallucination, perhaps induced by the great stress. She rested her head on her knees, nearly catatonic at the horrific sights before her.

"Human. You are in grave danger. The mana explosion caused by this ritual will, no doubt, be detected by the SCA. They will send a cleanup team here to incinerate any evidence and silence any witnesses. If you remain here, your best hope is being shot. Your worst possibility is to be kept as a test subject, constantly poked and prodded, injected with thamaturgical substances and eventually dissected when you inevitably succumb to their experiments. You need to move. Now."

The voice was insistent, but the utter terror Iris felt, as well as the agony of something deep inside her burning, made it difficult for her to listen. All she heard was that bizarre scraping noise, like sheets of sandpaper trying to make words.

"Human. MOVE." The words shook her to the core of her being, causing her to jump. Finally, she obeyed, shakily rising to her feet and peering out the window. Around six or seven sleek black vans and SUVs pulled up out front. Men and women in all-black tactical gear, toting bizarre weapons resembling assault-rifles with large discs jutting out to the side of the upper receiver poured out, securing the perimeter of the building. After them came a single man in attire even stranger than the dead cultists.

He stood around 170 centimeters in street clothes, a brown leather jacket left open to expose light body armor. His hair was short, messy and brown, leaving exposed piercing blue eyes and a large, jagged scar across his face. They darted around, seeking any possible threat. In his gloved left hand, he carried a simple wooden scabbard, the curved shape making Iris think it was a katana. Strangely, he carried no other weapons, sharply contrasting the modern military look of the others.

As the troops flowed forth, he barked out orders, slowly walking forward himself. The grating voice yelled once more. "Human. Run! Not to them, out the back. I will aid you." Though still terrified beyond belief, Iris obeyed, turning away from the men and rushing for the exit. Her boots splashed in the blood of the cultists as she moved towards the entrance she used when she found this building. Finally, she reached it, turning the handle and pushing the door open with her shoulder.

Thankfully, the soldiers had not yet reached the back of the building. As such, she searched the backstreet for a path away from them. The only exits she saw were down the street and into two different crossroads, likely already secured by them. If she stayed here, however, it would only be a matter of time before she was seen.

"Climb the wall. The alleyways will hide you."

It was past her height, and being out of physical shape, she wouldn't be able to do that easily. Nevertheless, she knew the voice was right. It was her best hope. Looking around for anything that could help her, she noticed a few trash cans. Seizing one, she upturned it and placed it against the wall, climbing onto it and taking hold of the concrete.

Iris strained her muscles to the limit, but couldn't scale the wall. Another shock of pain enveloped all of her arms' muscles, forcing them to contract. Gritting her teeth, she lifted up her legs, crudely scaling the wall and dropping down. She looked downward, observing her muscles spasming and slowly relaxing. After this, they were extremely sore.

"I said that you'd have my aid."

That damn voice again, with no apparent source, nor an explanation as to what had happened. Still, Iris could only take the time to question it if she escaped the situation she was in. Looking around, she knew that her best hope was to get lost in the maze of alleyways. In a brisk jog, she picked a path at random and set off, hoping she would have a chance to rest soon. She was quite exhausted and had a lot to process.

After a few minutes, she slowed to a stop, falling to her knees. Even with that, it wasn't the end of her troubles.

"Human, do not rest in the open. You are covered in blood and they will find you." Much to her chagrin, the voice was right. As before, she looked around for nearby objects. Old furniture, piles of weeds from someone doing yardwork and a discarded washing machine weren't of much use to her. She did, however, find something that could hide her; a dumpster. Thankfully, she could stand on the handles this time, allowing her to climb into it much more easily.

Laying down, she closed the lid above her and finally rested. Her lungs, burning for oxygen, were further tortured by the smell of rotting trash. Nevertheless, she finally had her time to rest. With little other recourse, she closed her eyes, tears streaming down her face.

CHAPTER 2: ESCAPE

"Human. What is your name?"

Once more, the voice asked her. Iris was extremely uncomfortable answering it, but it had helped her escape. But nevertheless, she was extremely ambivalent about responding. It was likely the creature which had assumed her father's shape, after all.

"...Iris," she muttered, her voice echoing in the dumpster. This caused her to note that the thing's voice had no such echo.

"Iris," it repeated, enamored. Her sense of revulsion grew at its doting tone. "Listen to me. We have narrowly escaped capture by the SCA for now, but we remain in grave danger. Though they will not continue their search openly, they will absolutely seek to account for interlopers. It is very likely you were seen fleeing and it is only by sheer luck that we have escaped. Your clothes are drenched in blood, which will, no doubt, be reported by anyone who sees you. We need to plan our next move."

Laying in the dumpster, Iris desired nothing more than to curl up and cry. She had lost the only family she had and now she was being pursued by some black operations unit. Ultimately, however, the thing was right. She was not safe here. Biting her lips to stave off the tears, she began thinking.

Could she simply pay for a ride? She removed her phone from her pocket, but thought twice. Any Ridr driver would likely call the police if they saw a young woman covered in blood seeking their services. Anyone she could call for help? The police were out, as they were likely connected to that unit in some fashion. Nor did she have any friends who could help her. Her prospects looked dim. Her further thoughts were interrupted by the voice again.

"Discard that phone. Now."

Logically, it was right. Even when turned off, phones could be tracked and Iris did not know how far their reach extended. However, she didn't want to get rid of it entirely, so she removed the battery.. It may have been better to simply break it and leave it behind, but even under such dire circumstances she held an attachment to the device, paid for by her own labor and with a great amount of customization.

The question of what to do remained. Iris could not remain in this dumpster forever and simply walking home in this condition was out of the question. So, she resolved to find another set of clothes as soon as she could. With a grunt of effort, she pushed open the lid, observing her surroundings. As before, she was alone in the dumpster, but she noted the light was gradually dimming. A mixed blessing, as the darkness would make it harder to see the blood but also more difficult to navigate the unfamiliar territory.

Stepping out, she found herself in a business district. She vaguely remembered going here with her father for a burger a couple weeks ago. Closing her eyes, she thought over her memories, trying to remember any businesses which might be useful. A hardware store, fast food restaurants and a gas station weren't likely to help her. Then she remembered a thrift store which sold donated clothing. That would be useful.

The fact remained that anyone seeing her was likely to call the police. Due to this, she'd have to raid the donation bin. In this situation, covered in blood and grime from a dumpster, she could hardly afford to be picky. Sticking to darker areas in the hopes of remaining unseen, she walked to the bin and tested the lid. "Locked. Shit." Why did they bother locking a donation bin for a thrift store? What kind of scumbag would steal old, worn out clothes meant to help the poor? Oh, right. Her.

Well, she had a way around that. Namely, the set of lockpicks she carried in her pocket for the sake of fulfilling her occasional flash of curiosity and sense of exploration. As she got to work, the voice spoke up again.

"Why do you have those?"

Ignoring it, Iris finished her work and popped the lid open. The lock stood no chance against her experienced hands. After vaulting into the bin, she tossed out a few trash bags which she thought might be promising. Jumping out after them, she got onto her hands and knees and tore them open, hoping to find something that fit her.

Unfortunately, they were mostly kid's clothing with one larger pair of worn pants and a denim jacket. Iris surmised that some construction worker donated his old clothing after buying a new set. None of those were suited to her, but given the situation, she hardly had time to search for something else. She looked extremely suspicious as it was, so she simply took the pants and jacket and ducked behind the bin.

"Put your old clothes in the bin. It will help to erase any traces."

After Iris finished changing, she grabbed her phone, wallet and keys from her old jeans, placing them into her new ones. The donated clothes were replaced and her old outfit joined them. Now, she looked bizarre, a 15 year old girl in men's clothing with huge bags under her eyes and a dull stare. But that was far, far better than looking like she just walked out of a murder scene. Her stomach growled.

Looking around, Iris spotted a solution to that problem. A nearby fast food place, and perhaps, a way home, as well. Walking once more, she crossed the street and pushed open the doors. Two bored-looking young men behind the counter stopped talking and turned toward her, their eyes opening.

Finally, one spoke. "...Holy crap, lady, you alright? I can call the cops if you need me to."

Fuck. Iris suddenly realized that it wasn't just her clothes that were covered in blood, but her hands, as well. A bit of it somehow got splashed on her face and she was still wearing the same shoes. Thinking quickly, she thought of an excuse. "I'm fine. I was helping the paramedics at a car accident a few blocks away and haven't had the opportunity to shower," said Iris.

The men looked skeptical, but didn't press the matter further. "...Well, then, may I help you?" he asked.

"...Yes. A cheeseburger, large fries and a large soda, please," she said.

"One moment." After she paid, Iris sat down and contemplated her next actions. She couldn't safely use her own phone, but she could certainly use someone else's. As she thought over her next steps, her food was placed in front of her. Quietly, she muttered her thanks before eating. As expected after what she saw, her food was bland and tasteless.

Iris, nevertheless, forced it down her throat. An empty stomach wouldn't help matters. She tossed the wrappers into the trash and walked up to the counter once more. Thankfully, the place was deserted, which would make this conversation a bit easier.

"Listen, uh, my phone's dead and my house is a few miles away. I'll give you twenty bucks if you let me use yours to call a ride," said Iris.

"I brought a spare charger. I could just give you that," said the young man. He was certainly kind, though Iris wasn't sure if it was because he wanted to help her or he thought she'd simply take his phone and run. Thinking along those lines, Iris put her wallet on the counter, as though to say 'Here's collateral that I won't just bail', before speaking again.

"No, I mean, my phone's dead dead. It won't even turn on." As proof, Iris pulled it out and held the power button. Nothing. Turns out removing the battery was a smart idea in more ways than one. She put it back into her pocket and glared expectantly. The young man turned to his friend, who nodded. He decided to trust her and handed her his phone. Iris opened her wallet, but the man spoke up. "Keep your money. You've had things rough as it is."

"...Thanks." That finished, Iris ordered herself a Ridr and stepped outside. As she breathed in the cool night air, she struggled to keep her composure. Her own father was dead. She was alone. Well, save for that voice which kept interjecting itself. Even after she got home, what was she going to do? She was never confident enough to pave her own way, she simply saw problems and did her best to patch them over. In sorrow, she closed her eyes.

Honk honk. Iris opened her eyes and saw a scratched up old station wagon before her, a large black man in robes and a turban sitting in the driver's seat. Under any other circumstance, she would be amused at the stereotype, but not now. Not now. Silently, her eyes dull, she opened the back door and stepped in, staring out the window.

For a couple minutes the driver was silent, out of courtesy or out of disinterest, Iris could only speculate. At least, that's what she thought until he spoke. "Are you alright, lady? Need me call police?" he offered. His voice was heavily accented and his Aenglic broken, but he showed concern, nevertheless. "...I'm fine, thanks," she muttered, disinterestedly, before resorting to her previous lie. "Helped out some paramedics. Changed my clothes but haven't showered."

In the window, Iris faintly saw her own reflection for the first time tonight. Her short brown hair was caked in blood, far more than she had thought, while the huge bags under her eyes and the dull stare were reminiscent of a teenage drug addict. Forcibly, she turned her head away, instead staring at her similarly dirty shoes.

Grimacing at that, as well, she simply closed her eyes instead and exhaled heavily.

Eventually, after agonizing minutes, the car arrived a few blocks away from her apartment building. Iris peeled herself out of it and waited for it to leave for another passenger before she walked off. It was a pointless precaution, all things considered, but she didn't want to make the job of that black-ops unit any easier. That in mind, she began walking.

CHAPTER 3: RETURN

The streets were filled with cars zipping past her, some late workers, others going grocery shopping. The crowd provided Iris a sense of strength in numbers, that being, she was now harder to pick out. If she weren't captured or killed by now, it's unlikely she would be. Her muscles ached and trembled, but she forced herself onward. Biting her lip, she only further resolved herself to make it back.

Make it back to her empty apartment building filled with the possessions of a man killed by some cult for reasons unknown. Once more, Iris trembled as she remembered the grotesque scene she saw, where blood flowed like a river. For a moment, she stopped, falling to her knees and feeling tears run down her face.

"Iris. Keep moving," said the voice.

The damn voice again. Iris obeyed, picking herself up and continuing onward. In a few more minutes, she arrived at her building, a nondescript brutalist monstrosity that looked straight out of an Eastern European country ravaged by political instability. On worn stairs she climbed before arriving in front of her door and turning the knob. Locked, of course. She pulled her key from her pocket and turned it, stepped in and closed the door behind her.

Before her laid the fruits of her labors, luxury furniture and hardware ordered piecemeal from various auction sites. A large TV was bolted against the wall, flanked by large custom speakers. Beneath it, a metal entertainment console with CDs, movies and other forms of media. Perhaps most notable was a small computer, around the size of a textbook, laid beneath it. Paired to it, a wireless mouse and keyboard lay on top of a worn coffee table lying in front of a white stuffed down couch. At either end of the couch were recliners, one grey, one black, picked by her and her father according to preference.

Almost expecting to see her father, Iris walked to his chair, before being slammed with the horrid recollection of what she had seen. She collapsed into it, holding her knees to her chest and sobbing once more. "Dad... Daddy," she sputtered out, whimpering. After a few minutes, the soreness deep within her body, as well as occasional shooting pains, forced her to lay down. It was all she could do to muster the will to pull the recliner's lever before laying down and drifting to sleep.

Despite her harrowing circumstances, Iris had a rare eight hours of sleep. She woke up feeling rested, but devastated, remembering the events of yesterday. Her next feeling was hunger, a reminder that she needs to fulfill her biological needs in spite of her emotional turmoil. Briefly, she considered getting up, but couldn't muster the will. How could she? She wouldn't find her father in the kitchen making her breakfast. She couldn't make anything for him. It was just her now.

She closed her eyes, too despondent to do anything else. The voice, though, wasn't going to let her rest.

"Iris. You need to eat. If you are not able to find yourself something, order a pizza. The danger may not have subsided, and you cannot evade your enemies with an empty stomach," ordered the voice.

"What are you?!" she exclaimed. Enraged, Iris grabbed a nearby object and threw it at a bookshelf. She noticed it was a pillow as it knocked over a few technical manuals then settled on the floor. Even after all this, that thing was still talking to her?!

"...A demon. I will answer any and all questions you have, but you must promise not to panic," it said.

Is this some kind of sick joke? It wouldn't leave Iris alone even after this? Given what she had seen yesterday, and that bizarre paramilitary squad, she presumed that the term "demon" wasn't a metaphor for something else. Sighing, she took her head in her hands and shuddered before removing her phone from her pocket.

Black screen. Iris replaced the battery. A couple notifications from messaging apps and games, but nothing important. Feeling too exhausted to put a lot of time into it, Iris opened a fast food app and repeated her last order. She'd have her food soon.

Iris's arm dropped limply to her side. Nothing had changed. She was still in stolen clothes, laying in her father's chair and covered in blood and sweat. Well, on that note, it would be extremely problematic if a delivery worker saw her in this condition. So, she forced herself upward, intending to retrieve an outfit and take a shower.

She headed for her familiar room, the largest room in the house, but decided against it. It was a pizza, not a job interview. Not that she'd ever had one of those, of course, but the sentiment remained. That in mind, she forgot about retrieving anything more formal, grabbed a bathrobe from the hall closet and took it with her to the bathroom. Her stolen clothes were discarded, as she had no reason to keep a soiled, worn out outfit meant for grown men.

Though Iris typically enjoyed the hot water, she was now apathetic to it, her attention commanded more by the disgusting colors running down into the drain. Streaks of red were the most common, of course, but occasionally, they mixed with putrescent yellows and greens from bile that had dried into her hair. Her body had soaked up more viscera than she had expected, much to her revulsion. Grabbing a bar of soap, she morosely scrubbed at herself.

"When you finish, hide those clothes. Is there an incinerator nearby? We need to burn them," said the voice.

"How are you talking to me, demon? Who are you? Why won't you leave me alone?" she sputtered out. Iris was infuriated by this thing's continued presence. She held her short brown hair in her hands, trying not to break down once more at this absurdity. The demon spoke.

"...I am inside you. I forcibly contracted you in order to aid you in escaping from the SCA. As for who I am, I am Merkuroth, the Lord of Worms, a Third-level Pseudo-Demon compounded into my current form upon death. There is, at the moment, no way for me to leave. If that is the route you wish to pursue, you need to-"

Knock knock. The front door of her apartment was rattled, causing Iris to jump. Thinking it best not to greet the delivery driver nude, Iris turned off the water and grabbed her worn grey bathrobe. It was her father's old one but he certainly wouldn't be using it any more. Without bothering to towel herself off, she put it on and walked out of the bathroom.

"Wait. Iris, it's only been a few minutes since you entered the shower. DO NOT OPEN THAT DOOR," commanded Merkuroth.

Iris failed to register Merkuroth's words in time. In front of her stood two men, one vaguely familiar. At first, she noted their police uniforms, then, their faces. The man in front was around 170 centimeters with piercing blue eyes, boring deep into her. Across one of them was a massive scar, as though his face had been hacked open with a machete. Bizarrely, he carried a collapsible baton perpendicular to his left hip. His partner, however, was shorter, at around 150cm, with a dull, bored look on his face.

"Hello, I'm Lieutenant James O'Flannigan with the Keras Police Department. My partner is Sergeant Keith Bankowitz. Are you Iris Kriemhild?"

Merkuroth spoke. "Repeat after me. Yes, I am. What is your business here?"

"...Yes, I am. What is your business here?" Iris obeyed. She wasn't used to dealing with traditional authority figures, much less ones that lead bizarre black-ops squads. Clearly, however, they had come in a police disguise for a reason, and she had hoped it wasn't one that involved her own assassination.

"We're investigating the disappearance of a man named Hans Kriemhild. I believe he was your father. We'd like to ask you a few questions. May we come in?" asked James.

Merkuroth guided her reply once more. "...I'd rather not have you inside. There's a lot of half-completed electronics projects around and very little space. We can speak out here," said Iris. The demon further explained his words to her. "Do not turn your back on them and do not let them inside. You are vulnerable when you do not see them and when you are not in public," said the demon. She suppressed a shudder, knowing that these men were very likely familiar with the process of silencing inconvenient witnesses.

"Very well, then, though I assure you, it's not a bother. Your personal projects are not our concern, Hans is. That said, when was the last time you saw your father?" asked James. Keith pulled out a notepad and a pen, ready to take notes. On more advice from Merkuroth to give an innocuous answer, Iris told a half-truth. "Yesterday, my father and I visited the nearby Happy Hills theme park. When I got back from a roller coaster, I couldn't find him. I found no luck searching or asking at the help desk. Calling him just got me an answering machine. I had little recourse at that point so I got a Ridr home, thinking I'd come up with something else tomorrow," said Iris. This was, of course, leaving out the part where she tracked down his phone and came upon that grisly scene.

"That also answers my second question of where you were on that day," said James. It seems he had a sense of humor, though Iris doubted that was his real name. "When was the last time you saw him? And when did you get home?"

"Around 5, I'd say. I would recommend checking the logs at the park," said Iris. In truth, it was exactly 1704 hours, but she had no interest in placing suspicion on herself for knowing the precise times. "As for getting home, around midnight."

"We'll definitely be following up with the park and nearby businesses, see what we can dig up. We'll do everything we can to get your father back to you," promised James. That was total bullshit, Iris thought. They were cleaners, not investigators. "Next question, do you know anywhere he might have gone? A motel he liked, a relative, a friend?" Iris thought for a moment. "Hrm, no. My grandparents are assholes, so that rules them out," she said. Keith smirked at her candor. "We barely ever had any fights or anything. I don't know about his friends or coworkers, you might have better luck asking at Solar Panorama. He was an accountant for them. Wait, why are you here after only a day?"

Clearly, James was a bit taken aback by her inquiry. "Er, the park reported his disappearance and forwarded it to us," said James. Knowing everything that had happened, that clearly wasn't the only factor at play. Iris, however, wasn't stupid enough to say so out loud. "Anyway, next question. Did he have any enemies? Jilted lovers, estranged coworkers, that sort of thing?" Keith furiously scratched at his notepad. She was extremely curious what he was writing, but wasn't stupid enough to try to swipe it from him.

"...No. My mother died in a car accident when I was very young. He had a boyfriend for a while, but they separated on amicable terms since he wanted to have kids and my father was happy with just me," said Iris. Keith smirked at her statement. Iris clenched her jaw, suppressing the urge to punch him. Interrupting her anger was a very tall, muscular woman in a red uniform climbing up the stairs to her apartment and walking toward the trio. "Food's here!" she shouted, which irritated Iris more.

How serendipitous to have an excuse to take a break from the interrogation. All three turned to the woman, but James spoke next. "We were just about done here. Enjoy your meal, and take this." He took a business card out of his pocket and held it out to Iris. She glanced at it, seeing the words "Lieutenant James O'Flannigan, Keras Police Department" in front of an indentation of the KPD's snazzy minimalist sword and shield logo. The two cleaners began walking off, leaving Iris alone with the delivery worker. As Iris reached up and took the food, the worker stared down at her. "Jeez, what's with them? Haven't ever delivered to a cute girl getting lectured by cops before. Well, maybe once!"

Quite irritated, Iris nevertheless understood it's typically best to just give people what they want if you want them to leave. "My father disappeared. They're investigating." She took the food and the pen to sign the receipt. The delivery worker, however, kept talking. "Oh, that's not good. You know, my brother once disappeared for a couple weeks. He had just turned 18 and my parents were really overprotective, so they ended up calling in search teams. Search teams, just for a kid who went on a road trip! He wasn't stupid or anything, just wanted to do something new with his life. Everyone does something fun when they turn 18, but my parents just couldn't understand that. Instead they-"

Growing tired of her ranting, Iris grabbed the pizza and receipt before slamming the door in her face.

CHAPTER 4:
QUESTIONS

Morosely, Iris sprawled across the couch and began eating her pizza. Anchovies and olives, her favorite. But she couldn't enjoy it, not now. Mechanically, she shoveled it down, concerned only with her biological need for sustenance. After getting halfway through her food, she spoke. "Are you still there?"

"I am always with you," said the demon in its disturbing, grating voice. More unsettling than that, however, was his statement. That was, however, not Iris' prime concern at the moment.

"Who were those men?" asked Iris.

"They were agents of the SCA, sent to assess your knowledge level of the incident and pass on information to their superiors. At the moment, you are not considered a prime suspect. If you were, you would either be dead or in their custody." Iris shuddered at the thought. She certainly wasn't entirely on the right side of the law, but she had no interest in antagonizing some extralegal black ops unit. "The one calling himself James O'Flannigan is actually named Francis Sullivan. James O'Flannigan is simply an identity he uses during cover work with the KPD. He is an extremely dangerous man, a Water/Wind/Life/Light magus with great experience working with the SCA. Never turn your back on him and avoid him if at all possible. As for Keith Bankowitz, I am afraid I have no knowledge about him. My assumption is that he is a trainee within the Agency learning how to operate covertly from a veteran member."

"..." Iris mulled over the fact that the demon seemed to have prior experience dealing with this Francis Sullivan, as well as the strange way he was described. "I realized they weren't officers when I saw them because their pistols were non-standard, as well. Looked like UK-38s, though I didn't get a good look. The KPD issues Armko 19s. But anyway, tell me more about what you mean by water wind life light magus."

"You really don't know anything, do you?" said Merkuroth. No rancor was in the demon's words, simply a statement of fact. "Very well, then. As we know it, there are ten schools of magic; fire and water, earth and wind, life and death, light and shadow, and space and time. Those who are born with magic circuits are capable of acquiring five of these. Barring extremely rare circumstances, one cannot use both a school of magic and its opposite. Attempting to do so will cause your circuits to explode. All ten schools have different capabilities, providing resistance to the other as well as supernatural powers inaccessible to most people."

Iris had certainly had her conception of the world shattered as of late, but having supernatural phenomena confirmed to her was particularly disgusting. Cultists like the one she had encountered, a mysterious SCA and outright magic? There were many, many ways she could see things like this exploited against the common people, and indeed, she feared what else she was unaware of, given what she had seen. In spite of her apprehension, she pressed on. "Tell me about those cultists and how you came to inhabit my body. And this SCA. For that matter, was I born with magic circuits?"

"My past is... a very long story. I'll give you an abridgement for lack of time. I was one a half-human mortal in another world seeking to gain powerful dark magics. I succeeded, but found my body wracked with hellfire burns and reliant upon these very magics in order to survive. My psyche became twisted and I came to the conclusion that radical change was necessary for humanity to survive. This was, of course, a matter of some dispute and great sacrifice was needed.

Some, however, disagreed with the sacrifice I... imposed onto people, painting me as an enemy of all mankind. A role I had no reluctance in embracing, but one man in particular learned all he could about me. In a final confrontation, close to my ultimate goal, he overcame me in combat and executed me. This was, however, not the end. My scattered soul found itself in the aether, as with all the dead, and my extremely strong aptitude for said magics allowed me to retain my consciousness, and gradually, I became a Pseudo-Demon. In other words, a class of demons which were once mortal but achieved a different form by various means."

Merkuroth continued. "The cultists are one of a great number of groups in this world who stumble upon some scrap of arcane knowledge and think themselves special for it. In this case, the grandson of a very wealthy artist who, completely by accident, managed to discover a rune particular to me. Experimenting from there, he bound my coalescing form to a cheap costume dagger. Gathering like-minded friends with similar scraps unto himself, he formed the Cult of the Encroaching Shadow, seeking to establish themselves as a new power in the world."

"During this process, I learned all I could from the leader but quickly realized he was nothing more than an egotistical fool seeking lackeys and sycophants. Being near him was absolutely unbearable, but I used him as much as I could to learn about this world. Indeed, I see many similar patterns of history within it - the common presence of humans, the emergence of magic during the beginnings of catastrophe, conflicts between social classes based on material interests. I theorize that there is some innate starting point between this and possibly other worlds, but I digress entirely."

The pieces began to fit together, Iris thought, as she reviewed the moments leading up to that gut-wrenching scene. She spoke. "And you sought to escape this moron who fancied himself a cult-leader?"

"Indeed!" Merkuroth chuckled, an absolutely nauseating sound. "To do so, I goaded him towards finding another host, someone who could contain my power. I assured him - falsely, of course - that it would be trivial for him to control this host. As such, using his own meagre abilities, he began seeking a suitable one at crowded public places. Sports stadiums, shopping malls, and eventually, an amusement park."

"No..." Iris whispered, shuddering at the thought.

"I am sorry, Iris," apologized Merkuroth. He sounded absolutely sincere, but she had no way of knowing the truth behind his words. "My intention was never for the host to die. But rather, to lend them power to get away from those imbeciles and pursue their own goals. They, however, knew absolutely nothing about proper containment and imbuing rituals. Their mistakes killed your father, as well as themselves."

Despondent, Iris stared downward. She closed her eyes as the tears flowed down her cheeks once again. Her father died solely out of pursuit of power, not for any higher reason, but because he was simply unlucky enough to be compatible with this demon which now resided within her. Much as she hated to continue, there were still unanswered questions. "What of the SCA?" she asked. "What do you know about them, and how? You seem quite knowledgeable."

"The SCA is the Supernatural Containment Agency, a covert government institution seeking to control the emerging supernatural activity within your world," explained Merkuroth Quite a simple answer, Iris thought, but the demon continued. "They operate extralegally, outside the confines of the law and most apparatuses of the state. Indeed, they report directly to a council of elites within the government."

"So a secret police?" asked Iris. From her readings, though up until last night, not her experiences, Iris was familiar with such things.

"In a word, yes. However, they are strained beyond measure. Approximately one in sixty six people have some degree of magical ability, which makes information suppression alone an extremely intensive task. In addition to that, they are constantly being deployed to incidents which threaten to expose the public to the truth of the supernatural. Last night's ritual was merely one of many for them. Nothing more," said Merkuroth.

Iris shuddered at the latest disturbing revelation. Not only this disturbing agency, but the fact that one in sixty six, 1.15% of all people on this planet, were capable of defying conventional scientific knowledge in some way. She recalled from various studies she had read that institutional change was only possible if 3.5 percent of the population were willing to actively participate. Now, though, conventional society would have to undergo major changes in order to survive this new emergence. Changes she would soon live through. "But how do you know so much?" she asked once more.

"The same way any magi knows of them. Those with unusual abilities, both magical and otherwise, have a tendency to network with those like themselves and spread their own knowledge. The existence of the SCA is absolutely an open secret among the magi community and all but the most unintelligent and the most unlucky know to keep their heads down. The hand of the State is far more powerful than most magi, after all."

Disgusting. Iris was no anarchist, but she certainly was not comfortable with a secret police dedicated to enforcing control over people with these new abilities. But then, what should she do? What could she do? As a citizen, she had no influence over an extralegal organization. But as simply a private actor? "I asked before if I had magic circuits," she said.

"You do," said Merkuroth. Iris shuddered at the confirmation that she had the same abilities within her. "They are few and of poor quality. Your aptitude with magic will be forever limited. Save, of course, in the Shadow attribute, which you hold an extremely high affinity for. I heavily suspect you have trace demonic ancestry."

"You mean... I'm not human?! I'm a demon like you?" yelled Iris.

"Keep your voice down! You are human, mostly, but your genetics have been influenced in some way by another demon mating with one of your ancestors. If you wish to know more, I would suggest asking your parents, but I'm afraid that's no longer an option," explained the demon. Though he was not outright malicious, Merkuroth utterly lacked tact. "Your grandparents may also know something, but your conversation with the agents gave me the impression you do not wish to speak with them."

"Absolutely not," emphatically said Iris. Most of her questions were now answered. She knew what had happened to her father and why, what that strange unit was and the hidden crisis this world was facing. What was left, then? She would now live alone, which left her with no accountability, but also no guidance, save from this demon. But then again, how could she possibly trust it? "You're awfully forthcoming about all of this," she observed.

"Yes," said Merkuroth. Once more, he was curt and to the point. "I failed in my endeavor to change the world, thus, I am not worthy to be the one who does it. As such, I will gladly help you in whatever your endeavors may be, under two conditions. One, you cannot seek power solely for the sake of personal advancement. Two, you cannot harm the innocent without a greater cause for doing so." Absolutely bizarre. In stories she had read, demons were conniving, duplicitous beings, seeking to harm mortals for their own gain. And yet this one seeks to help her at personal expense. "How could I possibly trust you?" asked Iris.

"..." Merkuroth was quiet, likely mulling the question over. "The answer is complicated. If I had intended to harm you, it would have been trivial to do so. I could have let you be captured by the SCA unit. I could have forcibly taken control of your body. Or, indeed, I could simply force you to grab a kitchen knife and open your throat." Iris shuddered at the grisly image. "From that much, I hope you can at least trust I don't want you dead. As for my intentions, I've laid them out as clearly as I can. Should you not believe me, I can guide you to learning how to separate my immaterial form from your body, though it will be quite a process."

The prospect of doing so appealed to Iris, though rationally, she wasn't sure if that would be a wise choice. She was alone in a new world with only him as an ally, and removing him would cut off her sole source of knowledge and support. "I'll have to think about it," she resolved.

"Very well, then. But now, Iris Kriemhild, I have a question for you. What are you going to do?" asked the demon. "You have a power unavailable to most people, as well as an intelligence to overcome any obstacles in front of you. But to what end will you use them towards?"

That question was certainly not something Iris was prepared for. What should she do, then? A world of possibilities was now open to her. Should she dedicate herself to the destruction of the SCA? That would be extremely difficult, and she knew a power vacuum could result in the advent of something worse. Should she seek to eliminate those who would use similar demonic rituals? Slightly hypocritical, given that she was now bound with a demon, herself, but she enjoyed the idea. Should she seek to help people with her unusual abilities? Perhaps, but that would also entail attracting the attention of the SCA. In the end, her answer was "I don't know. I don't know, but I want to do something. And for that, I need more power."

"A wise answer. Do not rush headlong into your endeavors without preparation," cautioned Merkuroth.

CHAPTER 5: TRAINING

Yet another example of Hans' great love for Iris was her own living quarters. She had the master bedroom, with ample space for her numerous projects while her father had taken a much smaller room for himself. She realized she eventually had to clean out his room, but for now, she had other concerns. Shuddering at the thought of fully confronting his permanent absence, she looked over her living space. In each corner was a desk, each having different tools scattered on it. One had a set of padlocks and associated picks, another had scattered circuit boards, wires and an unplugged soldering iron. Yet another desk had a disassembled flip phone, some metal pipes and vials of differently colored powders scattered around. The largest one of all, however, had a massive desktop tower with an array of monitors and glowing technicolor peripherals. As she looked over the desks, Merkuroth spoke. "It was a very wise decision not to let those agents in. I am not familiar with the laws of Gamma but regardless, constructs like this would certainly invite suspicion."

He was right. "Regardless of whether they're smoke bombs or genuine IEDs, the authorities don't usually look very kindly on precocious young women building illicit gadgets." Particularly ones who also had a room with an extensive bookshelf filled with books with titles such as "The End of the State: The Individual in the Modern World", "The Development and Centralization of Capital" and "A History of Terrorism as Political Catalyst". Not to mention, all of the posters of obscure Eastlands animated media. But that was far from her primary worry right now. Collapsing on her king-size memory foam bed, she muttered, face down. "What do I do, Merkuroth?" She had lost so much, yet gained new, hidden knowledge.

The demon spoke once more. "I can offer only suggestions, not orders. Even a cursory glance at your room tells me you are quite intelligent and skilled in unorthodox abilities like clandestine engineering, chemistry and information gathering. What you lack, however, is physical strength and the ability to defend yourself. In your position, I would seek out self-defence and martial arts classes, as well as begin an exercise regimen. As you are now, you would succumb to anyone with even a modicum of experience."

Merkuroth was right. Iris had long neglected her body in favor of her other interests, and indeed, subsisted on a diet of fast food and energy drinks. Morosely, she turned over, looked down and grabbed a handful of flab on her stomach. That would have to go. As painful as it was to plan and move forward in these circumstances, she couldn't simply ignore it. Not if she was going to survive in this situation. Lethargically, she pulled herself up, moving to the desk with her computer and turning it on. After inputting a 30-character password, her screens flickered to life, illuminating her face in their glow. Setting aside several windows of other projects from IED schematics to programming tutorials to pork roast recipes, she instead looked into nearby gyms.

"Modern Fitness, hm? It has good reviews... What do you think?" She asked her demon. "Iris, I have no experience with how this society encourages physical fitness, save that it is far more materially enriched than mine. I saw very few obese people, and I learned to fight from rudimentary militia training and copying the movements and strikes of my myriad foes. I can only suggest you think critically." Perhaps it was not the wisest question on her part. In spite of that, she looked over the schedule and saw a women's night in one week's time. She registered to attend and paid the modest fee.

Progress. But what now? Iris' father is dead. That thought kept intruding into her mind. She could exercise, she could learn, she could perhaps even develop whatever bizarre abilities she might have. But there was nothing she could possibly do to change that fact which would forever be part of her life, now and forever. Shit. She lowered her head onto the desk and sobbed, tears and snot slowly running down her face. "Is he truly gone?" questioned Iris.

"I'm sorry, Iris. As yet, I know of no way to resurrect the dead," said the demon.

"As yet? Could a way be developed?" asked Iris. That would be a goal she would dedicate her life towards, regaining the father she had stolen from her. She would dedicate all of her resources - time, money, knowledge, - towards it. Was it possible?

"It is extremely unlikely. My knowledge in the fields of Life and Death is limited, but the body is gone and the soul was not captured. I'm afraid you have no recourse," said Merkuroth.

That just truly left her alone. Leaning her head back, she grabbed a discarded shirt and wiped her face. She didn't want to think about it, but if she spent the week until her training session researching and learning, she might be able to improve her skills. She lacked great financial resources as well as connections, so all she had was what she could teach herself. Lockpicking, hacking, constructing IEDs, she already knew these. But actual infiltration and combat? She wasn't naive enough to think her experience in video games meant anything in the real world.

Dragging herself away from her computer, she understood that she may as well start now. Healthy habits take effort, after all, and as it stood, she had a long way to go. After going to the living room, she lay prone and began doing pushups. After six, she stopped, rolling over to catch her breath.

"Good, very good, Iris." Merkuroth spoke. "You're showing a will to improve. Rest, then do six more." She complied, grunting with the effort, before collapsing. Afterwards, Merkuroth guided her through situps and instructed her to rest for the day. Covered in sweat, she took another shower, catching her breath as the warm water streamed over her.

What else did that leave? Iris' workout, as it were, was pathetic. Even so, difficult as it was, she needed to keep going. That's how she approached most problems in her life, simply setting a goal and finding a way to accomplish it. After exiting the shower, she rested for a half hour. She'd have more bad habits to drop if she wanted to find her path forward. So, she moved to the fridge, looking over her usual diet. Energy drinks, soda, frozen pizzas, burgers, a few frozen steaks her father would grill on special occasions. Most of it would have to go. She sighed, knowing that she would miss her lazy afternoons playing games and watching movies while gorging herself.

"What is most of this? I don't recognize these cylinders and rectangular packages," Merkuroth asked. "Food of some kind?"

"...You've never seen soda cans and frozen pizzas before?" asked Iris. She was bewildered for a moment, then realized precisely who she was talking to. She supposed such gaps in his knowledge were to be expected. He did spend time with the leader of that cult gathering information, but then again, he was likely rich enough to have food prepared for him. "Unhealthy foods. Easily prepared. I spent most of my time amusing myself so I didn't want to spend much effort cooking. That's going to have to change."

"All things considered, you're adapting very quickly. That is to be praised," said the demon. Iris wasn't sure whether to be pleased or disgusted with the complement. She decided to explain. "I'm going to train my body, and to do that, I'm going to need to eat better. Our country is so saturated with unhealthy food that obesity is one of our greatest health problems. I'm on the way to that, but I need to do things differently from now on."

As they spoke, Iris worked on trashing everything she once loved.

"You have so much food that even the common people face obesity? This world truly is different from mine." Mystified, he was silent for a few minutes, seemingly contemplating this information. Eventually, Iris broke the silence, tying up a trash bag as she spoke. "You really were isolated from day to day life inside that dagger, weren't you? It seems you'll be able to learn from me, as well."

"I look forward to it, Iris," said Merkuroth. Staring at her now nearly empty fridge, she realized she'd have to replenish it somehow. Usually, she had a habit of ordering everything online, but if she was going to change her lifestyle, she would start here. Thinking over her options, she realized she didn't have many. Her father's car? She couldn't drive, though she shuddered at the thought of another possession she now had forever associated with her dear father. A bike? Didn't have one, though it was a good idea. A Ridr? That would defeat the purpose. She'd have to walk for now.

Iris briefly wondered if she should be going outside right now but realized it would be more suspicious not to. In the SCA's mind, she was just some kid who lost her father and has no idea what really happened. So, Iris dug out a backpack from an old closet. It was mid-afternoon, which gave her plenty of time to get what she needed. What else would she need? A backpack, her lockpicks, a multitool. A water bottle, too. She wasn't planning on doing anything quite as severe as that night, but she knew those things were always good to have.

Her house keys, as well. Iris would need those. Properly equipped, she set out on her own, something she hadn't done for years. The streets were cracked and the buildings poorly maintained, but that didn't matter. It meant rent was cheap, and she wasn't going to get evicted anytime soon. Checking her phone, she found the grocery store was half a mile away. A bit much, but she'd take it slow and steady.

"No questions, then?" Iris asked Merkuroth. "No. The urban landscape is very familiar to me." That was bizarre. A demon from another world who found her own environment nothing significant. Just what kind of world did he come from? "I'll need to ask you all about where you're from, once I have no other priorities," she stated. "Indeed. Such knowledge may prove useful someday," he replied.

Iris continued on. The exercise was tiring, but novel to her. Eventually, she reached the store and stopped inside to rest. At a bench, she surveyed the aisles, employees and shoppers. "No questions here, either?", she asked. "Once more, none. I can extrapolate what I need from my own knowledge," he explained. His world must have had similar markets, since everyone needed to eat. He interrupted her thoughts with a confirmation. "I've been to many places like this before. The variety and packaging are quite different, however." In her own mind, she imagined a medieval market, with fruit stands, systems of weight for coinage and merchants yelling out to passing customers.

It took her around a half hour to grab what she needed. Though she had no set meal plan, she went heavy on vegetables and lean meats. From now on, things would be different. At Merkuroth's insistence, she loaded up on apples, as well. Ever the introvert, she went through the self-checkout and with a full backpack and hands full of bags, began walking home.

"How much control will you allow me?" asked Merkuroth. "We inhabit the same body and our sensation is shared. I wish to respect whatever limits you may set."

Iris froze. That wasn't something she had considered. The demon inhabited her and could control her as he wished. "...Don't do anything without me saying it's alright." That's all she could think of for now. "And especially don't stare at me while I'm getting dressed." Merkuroth was silent for a moment before chuckling. "Even if I were alive, I wouldn't proposition you. You're female. I prefer men." Well, if nothing else, that simplifies things. The implications of this could be pondered later.

Eventually, she reached her home and unpacked her things. Merkuroth was particularly excited when she got to the apples, imploring her to eat one. She eventually obliged, if only to shut him up, and he loved it. "What will I do now?" she wondered. It was early evening and she had time to kill before she'd go to bed.

As she often did when she was bored, she jumped onto her computer, booting up her favorite chat program Dissonance. As she began typing to one of her friends, Merkuroth interrupted her. "Don't. The SCA has eyes everywhere and will intercept your messages." That meant she couldn't talk to anyone but the demon? What a quandary. "What about the public information? You know, that my father is missing?" asked Iris. "That will work. Just be very careful with your messages," replied Merkuroth.

With no recourse, she instead told her friend all about the false story of her father's disappearance. Her theme park excursion, their separation, her solemn Ridr trip home. He was comforting, if somewhat dense. He never was one of her greatest friends, but certainly someone she'd talk to. What else was left for her? A dead father and a demon. Iris threw her head back and exhaled. Her entire world was different now, broken. Without the energy to do anything else, she crawled into bed and slept.

After Iris woke, four hours later, Merkuroth made a request. "May I show you something?" "What is it?", she asked. "Magic. You have the capability to use it, remember? I want to show you what you can do," he replied. The idea of it disgusted her, but if she was going to change things, prevent others from being sacrificed, she had to use everything at her disposal. "...Fine. Go ahead," said Iris. The demon raised her right arm in front of her. Then she screamed. Boiling hot lava mixed with shards of glass flowed through her veins, piercing her at every inch. She dropped to the floor, red-hot pokers stabbing every inch of her body. After an agonizing eternity, the pain slowly faded away, leaving her whimpering on the floor with a puddle of spit, tears and snot beneath her.

"I am sorry, Iris. There was no way to-"

"You're sorry? You're sorry? You're fucking SORRY? Do you have ANY idea what the fuck I just went through?" exclaimed Iris. More tears flowed at the sudden betrayal from him. "That was the worst pain I've ever experienced."

"Allow me to explain. Your magic circuits were dormant. You could not use magic. But by forcing mana through them, they are now active. You'll likely never experience that again, though your first few times using magic will be painful," explained Merkuroth.

"Mrrrgh." Iris grunted, slowly standing up. She'd have to clean up the floor later. With dread in her voice, she asked "What's next?" In reply, Merkuroth said, "This." He raised her right arm and pain shot through it once more. It felt like knives jabbing into it rather than lava flowing through this time. Her level of pain just below the limit of her tolerance, she instead focused on her hand. Strange polygons of shadow began emitting from it, cutting into the space around her before they coalesced into a smoky emission, somewhat like a car exhaust.

"You have the ability to manipulate shadows. Right now, this is all you can do. As your power grows, which I believe should not take long, you will gain the ability to cloak yourself in them and make them dense enough to resist enemy magics. Eventually, you may gain the ability to phase into the shadows themselves, which will be extremely useful for offense, defense and evasion," explained the demon.

Iris' new abilities were absolutely bizarre. "Is that all I can do?" she asked.

"For now, yes. You need to practice every day," explained Merkuroth. Iris winced at the thought of having to endure more pain. But she simply had no choice. Her abilities would grow over time and could not be rushed. "Tell me about the mechanics of magic. How does it work, what fuels it?" she asked.

"An excellent question," said Merkuroth. "To use magic, a magus must combine mana and an element before channeling it through their magic circuits. Without external guidance, learning this process is extremely difficult. As time goes on, their bodies will generate more and become attuned to it. Eventually, they may even assume elemental forms, changing their very essence." Iris pondered the information for a moment. "More basically, what is mana?" she asked. "An element, I can assume is something innate, given how I can already use Shadow. And what are magic circuits?"

"Mana is, as far as I know, a form of potential energy within the universe. It is typically a thin, ethereal substance, but can be gathered and compressed artificially into gaseous, liquid or solid forms, in order of density. Its physical properties change if an element is mixed with it, but it should always be considered volatile, dangerous and risky. Do not trifle with it," warned Merkuroth. And Iris now both contained and generated this substance within her body. It was like learning she was radioactive. The demon continued. "Elements are typically acquired artificially, for instance, through standing in a thunderstorm for days on end or remaining within pitch-black darkness for a week. In some cases, such as yours, people are born with an affinity."

So she was lucky. Or maybe not. As Merkuroth continued his explanation, Iris moved to the kitchen to grab a wet rag for the floor. "Magic circuits are, put simply, the organs which separate a magus from an ordinary person. As of yet, there is no means to artificially produce them, though I have heard rumors about harvesting and implanting them. Another abomination wrought by the SCA." Apparently, there were things even demons found disgusting. Now she understood the basics of magic. No doubt, there was much more to learn, but she could now use basic abilities.

Her next week was spent on self-improvement, exercising, eating a more nutritious diet and investigating, unsuccessfully, any rumors she could find of the SCA. Merkuroth told her they regularly scrubbed information from the Internet in order to maintain their secrecy. Due to that, magi typically communicated in person or with encrypted dead drops. Having no contacts, she had no one to learn from but him. One piece of information she found particularly interesting was that magi invariably ate a lot of food. Mana generation was theorized to relate to caloric consumption in some way, which meant she could eat as much as she wanted. Not that it was a very good idea to stuff herself with empty calories, of course, but her physical training took on a new aspect in light of this.

Eventually, the appointment for the women's self-defense class came. Realizing it was several miles away, Iris ordered a Ridr there. Her funds, while considerable, were not unlimited, so she silently made plans to figure out another method of transportation. It didn't take long to arrive at her destination; a small sports club. Leaving the car, she entered and was dismayed by what she saw.

"Are you fucking kidding me," Iris quietly muttered. The woman who delivered her pizza was sitting in front of a group of five women. She turned to walk around. "Wait. You need training, and this is a prime opportunity," said Merkuroth. "Mrgh," she grunted. "Fine." So, she turned back and joined them.

"Oh, hey, kiddo! I'm happy to see you here!" As before, she was irritatingly cheerful. Iris remained silent. "Did you find your father?" Once more, she was tempted to turn around and walk out, but Merkuroth cautioned her. "It has been a week. Do not become too angry with her."

"...No." Iris' explanation was short and left no room for argument. "Well, that's just too bad! I'm glad you're keeping busy, though.

It's good to keep doing things. Anyway, the name's Lydia Ope-line. I teach at this club, pizza's just a side gig for me. Most of the women here are newcomers, so it's good to see you!" Seeing as some of them were most certainly not engaged in exercise, or really, healthy living of any kind, that was no surprise. She was the youngest one there, which could be viewed many ways. Perhaps they didn't take their safety seriously, perhaps few younger people even saw the need.

"Let me show you girls a few things." With that, Lydia started the class. At Merkuroth's insistence, Iris volunteered as often as possible, hoping to learn as much as she could. Early on, most was just learning to either avoid or get out of trouble as rapidly as possible - don't go into dark alleys, travel in groups, let a friend know where you're going. Given that her plans were to explicitly pursue dangerous situations in the future, Iris found this to be of limited use. Afterwards, Lydia showed the class basic moves for incapacitating an attacker - eye gouges, elbows to the solar plexus, foot stomps and the occasional, venerated knee to the testes.

The class was productive, but not quite what she was hoping for. "Where can I learn something more offensive?" Iris asked. "Hrm, more traditional martial arts, perhaps?" replied Merkuroth. "Those are more offensive by their nature." They might also teach her the use of weaponry. Gamman law heavily restricted private arms ownership, but an intelligent person could always improvise some sort of damaging object. "Let's stop at the hardware store on the way back."

Once more, Iris took a Ridr to a nearby store and grabbed what she needed. A hammer, a few boxes of nails, some duct tape and a baseball bat might have made her look rather suspicious, but the bored teenage clerk, barely older than her, certainly wasn't about to say anything. Afterwards, she headed home, intending to get started.

"What are you doing, Iris?" asked Merkuroth. "Let me show you."

Setting up the bat on the coffee table, she first wrapped the end in duct tape to prevent it from splitting before hammering several nails through the end. "There. Cheap, easy to use and deadly," she explained. "Ah. I understand now. You've constructed a crude mace." He sounded unimpressed, which quite irritated her.

There was one more thing. Iris couldn't keep ordering Ridrs forever, especially considering she intended to engage in a lot of illegal activity. So, she pulled out her phone and started looking into potential vehicles. She couldn't drive, but she had options. Eventually, she settled on an electric bicycle which could either run silently off electricity or be pedaled. It should be maneuverable, easy enough to maintain and fast, which might end up saving her.

CHAPTER 6:
INVESTIGATION

The new bike arrived a week later. Iris didn't cry as often, but she still woke up from nightmares of what had happened. Her father's corpse, a writhing mass of flesh, silently reaching out at her. Covered in blood and gore, a grotesque monstrosity now sharing her body.. Shaking those thoughts from her mind, Iris turned to her new vehicle.

It was exactly as advertised, something quiet, fast and efficient. That in mind, she strapped on her helmet and took it out for a test drive. A flick of a switch on the handlebars switched it to the electric mode. "Someone attached an engine to this bicycle?" asked Merkuroth. "Sort of. It's just one mode, but you need to charge it and it doesn't give you any exercise," explained Iris. "That still sounds very useful," replied Merkuroth. "There's any number of things one could do with such a vehicle. I wish I had one in life."

Iris had a thought which made her apprehensive and a bit squeamish. However, she soon spoke up. "Want to try riding it?" Merkuroth was silent for a moment. "May I? I would love to, if you would permit me," he replied. "Well, go ahead, then," she acceded before relaxing her arms. He rapidly took control to prevent her from crashing before switching to the manual mode. "Your legs are fine and muscular, your lungs growing stronger, your heart more powerful than it was before." She blushed at the frank assessment of the state of her body. "I am, however, inexperienced in controlling a woman's body," he said.

Eventually, they decided to stop for food. Since Iris was exercising and because magi consumed so many calories, they didn't worry too much about her health when stopping for pizza. Merkuroth simply enjoyed the unfamiliar taste in silence as they ate. Afterwards, he spoke with another strange statement. "Iris, there's something I wish to show you," he said. "Can you go to a nearby humid area with dirt? Preferably one that's rained recently."

Now that was a strange request. Iris thought for a moment before pulling out her phone. "There's a park nearby. It's pretty run down," she explained. "That's fine," he replied. "Then let's go." With that, she got up, disposing of her trash and hopping on her new bike. Ten minutes later, they arrived, the equipment too damaged and the trees too decayed to host even the most humble of visitors.

"Let me show you what I mean. Thrust your finger into the ground and make a hole," Merkuroth requested. "W-what?" stammered out Iris. It took her a moment to realize he was speaking literally rather than in some sort of double entendre. She did as he asked, sinking her index finger into the wet soil. Within a few moments, she felt something welling up within her, like the magic she was learning to use but somehow different. Something like it was a part of her rather than some strange aberration grafted onto her.

In a radius of around 5 meters, hundreds of worms dug their way up through the soil and onto the surface. They squirmed, before abruptly stopping and gradually turning towards Iris. She shuddered at the sight, disgusted yet intrigued. "I am called the Lord of Worms for multiple reasons, but one of them is that I am capable of commanding the eponymous animals. Try it for yourself. Focus on your awareness spreading to them and command them to do as you wish," suggested Merkuroth.

"I always thought they were insects." said Iris, doing as Merkuroth asked. Immediately, they all began moving once more, crawling away from her and back into the dirt. "No. They're animals. I have read about them, but formal knowledge of such things was scarce in my world. Most of what I have learned came from my own experimentation. This ability is far more useful than you might understand. You can use it to store mana, to open locks, to create chemical reagents and even as an emergency food supply," said Merkuroth. Iris retched at the final suggestion.

Still, it was something she could do which few people would predict. That meant it would be prudent to establish a steady supply. After thinking over her apartment's available space, realizing she had her father's room empty now and feeling another wave of pain at his loss, she pulled out her phone and started ordering eggs and equipment for her own worm nursery. Most people use such things for composting, but for her, the worms were the end goal. But at any rate, she could also use her old food scraps to feed them since she was just tossing them out anyway.

After that was accomplished and she regained her emotional balance, Iris hopped on her bike and began pedaling home. It wasn't a long distance, but she was tired after so much biking. Eventually, they arrived and she collapsed into the chair in the living room. After a couple minutes, Merkuroth spoke. "Iris, what are your plans now?" he asked. "My... plans? I guess I'll get stronger. Figure out more about magic. And eventually clean up my father's stuff," she said. She still wasn't looking forward to the last one.

"Hmm." Merkuroth was silent for a moment then spoke again. "What do you want to learn?"

"That cult. The one that sacrificed Dad to summon you. How would I go about destroying them?" asked Iris.

"Now that is quite a goal! The high leadership was mostly wiped out, as you saw. The lay members, not so much. They might be captured and indoctrinated by the SCA, they might form a new sect of their own, or they might wisely retreat from the world of magic entirely. At any rate, the cult, as I knew it and as your father experienced it, will never exist in the same form," explained Merkuroth.

Iris almost felt bad she couldn't take them down herself. But what does that leave? "In that case, I think I want to investigate them for myself. Learn more about them, maybe get some sort of meaning from all this. If I even can," she said.

"Are you sure about that?" questioned Merkuroth. "You could easily run into the SCA again, and you barely escaped last time." Iris thought for a moment before speaking. "Yes. Yes, I'm sure. I'll figure more out when I get there. For now, can you help me figure it out?"

"Certainly. In your position, I would proceed by preparing my arms and equipment then showing up in the dead of night to their headquarters. I was housed there for quite some time, but the SCA likely will not have had the opportunity to investigate just yet. In all likelihood, the only reason they could intervene after my summoning was due to detecting a great amount of mana," said Merkuroth.

"Let's do it," resolved Iris. After resting for around an hour, she began putting together what she needed. Her lockpicks, of course, always useful for getting into places where they didn't want you to. Black clothing, to obscure herself in the darkness and disguise her identity. An old mask from a Halloween costume helped with that. Her old school backpack, from when she attended a physical school, in order to carry any supplies she needed. And, of course, her newly created nail bat, which should be a dangerous weapon even in her amateur hands.

Everything put together, she looked up maps of the facility online and began making plans. At around 1 AM, she'd use her bike to approach the area, stash it nearby and proceed on foot. After that, she should be able to infiltrate the building and hopefully find what she needed. If she even could find something that could help her make sense of her horrible situation. She usually barely slept, and when it came, it was only for a few hours, so being awake at the specified time would not be an issue.

That left Iris with several hours to herself. "Hmm," she thought to herself. "Weapon, check. Bag, check. Vehicle, check. Tools, check. What else can I do?" she asked. Merkuroth spoke. "Your magic is somewhat advanced from when you first acquired it. Why not attempt to cloak yourself in shadow? It may be useful in combat or to prevent identification." That was quite a suggestion.

Iris put both of her arms before her and began channeling Shadow-attribute mana through her magic circuits. Strange polygons of shadow began emitting from her outstretched hands before coalescing into that same bizarre smoke-like shape. It was still painful, but much less so. Easily manipulating the shadow, it slowly enveloped her body, leaving her a strange humanoid figure. Oddly, her vision was utterly unaffected. She stared at herself in the bathroom mirror. "How long can I maintain this?" she asked.

"I'd estimate around three hours. Which is extremely impressive for someone who has as little experience as you," said Merkuroth. Her demonic ancestry, perhaps? Just how far back did it go? "With time and effort, your abilities will only grow. But for now, bear this in mind. Your shadow can also be used to dampen the effects of magic. Very useful for fighting enemy magi," he explained. As ever, she resolved to develop that ability as far as possible.

First thing was to contact some people and purchase a few illicit encryption codes. With Iris' darknet connections, that really wasn't an issue. After that, she ate a meal, read one of her books and drank some diet soda. At 12:30, Iris was ready to head out. So, she gathered her belongings and walked out of her apartment building, mounting her bike and speeding towards the cult headquarters. It was an old, heavily fortified mansion, perhaps prepared by those who feared an imminent apocalypse, perhaps a billionaire's weekend getaway. Either way, it wasn't difficult to reach, even if it was on the outskirts of Kyras. She locked her bike up to a nearby bush, concealing it within the branches, before walking towards the headquarters.

There was a concrete wall around the mansion, the gate secured by an electronic keycard lock, but Iris had prepared for that. She used a flathead screwdriver to pop off the cover of the keycard scanner then pulled out a small tablet. Afterwards, she attached a cord to it and began poking at her device. Within a few minutes, the gate silently unlocked and Iris put her tools back into her backpack. "Very impressive, Iris," complemented Merkuroth. "You truly are prepared for something like this."

"Yeah, well, a lot of dipshits think that electronics will protect them. Truth is, there's always a person willing to sell a few security holes on the darknet for a couple Ripcoins." Iris' philosophy was proven correct by the open gate she strode through. Afterwards, she walked to the front door and easily picked it open. "Looks like we're in," she muttered. "Careful, Iris," cautioned Merkuroth. "You're in enemy territory. It appears to be abandoned, but it could still be dangerous."

Iris realized that she had absolutely no trouble seeing in the dark. "Is night vision a benefit of the Shadow element?" she asked. "Yes. Good deduction," said Merkuroth. "As you become more attuned to various attributes, your body will mutate as a result of hosting them. Generally, these mutations are beneficial, but all magi seek to hide them to avoid attracting the attention of the SCA." So, as a result of experimenting with the magic she had discovered as a result of hosting Merkuroth, she became a mutant. But then again, wasn't every living organism a mutant due to evolution? She put those thoughts aside, thinking she'd ask him more about what to expect later.

At this point, Iris realized that the mansion was rather large. Though certainly not on the level of a military bunker, she had no idea where she could go other than randomly wandering. And given that what she wanted to find was likely to be very well hidden, it very likely wouldn't lead her to it. "Fuck," she muttered. "Merkuroth, do you have any suggestions? I have no idea where I should go." He gave a mocking laugh. "Hah! Perhaps you should have thought of that before you decided to infiltrate this place. But no matter. I have some experience. First, you'll want to proceed to the security room."

Following his instructions, Iris walked down the halls. Though she had no trouble seeing ahead of her, the silence was, nevertheless, extremely eerie. After a few minutes of walking, she reached the room he specified and easily picked the lock. Inside, she found an array of monitors displaying security camera footage, as well as a wall full of keys. Most important, however, was the safe on the wall. "Code is 26-9-05. Some people think it wise to set it to their birthday." His guidance was astute. The safe popped open, revealing some gold coins, a bundle of money and a few flash drives.

"Check the false bottom. Those are worthless compared to what you're looking for," said Merkuroth. Well, how was Iris supposed to get into the bottom? Merkuroth didn't think it important enough to give further guidance, so she set aside the valuables and began prying at it with her flathead screwdriver. After a moment, she managed to hook it the right way and it slid right off, revealing a card with a magnetic stripe on one end. "I'm assuming this is what we're after," she said. "Yes, precisely. I would highly suggest replacing the valuables," guided the demon. "They're merely bait for any infiltrators." Silently, Iris replaced the bottom, the valuables then shut the door. It pained her to leave so much behind, but wealth wasn't what she was after.

"So you're saying someone carried you around in a costume dagger while they set up all this," said Iris. She was quite irritated at the thought of someone who thought themselves clever yet didn't think about the demon at their hip. "Precisely," said Merkuroth. "Now, you're heading for a bathroom closet on the ground floor. Go left, then go right, and bring your screwdriver." In another few minutes, she reached her destination. "Back of the closet, move the giant painting. Swipe the keycard and you're in." In to where, precisely? Iris surmised she'd find out.

After swiping the keycard, she heard a hidden door groan and slide open. Beneath her was a staircase heading straight downward for around a dozen meters, and at the bottom of that, another door. She began trudging down the steps one at a time, anticipating what she might find. Would it be more human sacrifices, making her their rescuing hero? Would it be tons of esoteric books on sorcery, granting her great power? Or perhaps it would simply be a meeting place for, as Merkuroth put it, amateurs who discovered scraps of knowledge and thought themselves great mages.

As it turned out, the answer was none of these. Iris pushed open the door on the bottom and found a room full of five SCA agents, clad in black military gear with those strange rifles on the back, complete with odd circular devices jutting out from the receivers. Leading them was Francis Sullivan, wearing the same brown leather coat, light armor underneath and the katana at his side. "Sweep and move, I don't want these bastards to have anything left behind. And make sure you watch out for- Iris?"

She froze, staring at the room full of operatives. Merkuroth, instead, took control, grabbing hold of her nailbat and swinging it at Francis's head. In a flash, he drew his katana, batting aside the weapon before pulling into a slash at her wrist. He jumped back, glancing up at the stairs to see that the hidden door had automatically shut. In a strangely kind tone of voice, Francis spoke to her. "There's no escape, Iris. You're in a room with four hostile soldiers and an extremely experienced magus. Your instincts are admirable, your execution, not so much. Drop the bat."

Merkuroth's answer was to activate all of Iris' magic circuits, once more flooding her body with Shadow-attribute mana and cloaking her body in darkness. Being a silhouette made it more diffi-cult for Francis to see Iris and though her body was not trained for melee combat, Merkuroth certainly was. He pressed forward, evading Francis's katana and striking with brutal, yet precise, blows. After deflecting one and evading another, Francis stepped backward, his katana becoming cloaked in blue and yellow flecks of light.

The demon in control of Iris' body kept low, stepping forward once more. He saw Francis strike forward, attempting another disarming maneuver. Merkuroth easily regained control of the bat and moved to strike at Francis but noticed the hand holding the bat flying through the air. His control slipped. Iris brought her arm in front of her, noticed the blood streaming out of her mutilated arm and screamed. Francis, however, showed no pity, viciously punching her solar plexus and throwing her to the ground. He kicked her in the stomach, causing her to vomit and sob in extreme pain.

"You've been in a fight before, but never a fight against a magus. You just don't understand what they're capable of," said Fran-cis. An experienced leader, he immediately switched to giving orders. "Garcia, treat her arm. Ice it. Satou and Hill, search her afterwards. I don't want another incident against someone who might be less prepared." Wordlessly, they began doing as they were told. Iris was barely aware of what was happening as she was carried to a spare room to have her bloody arm bandaged so she wouldn't bleed out. Afterwards, the two female operatives re-moved her clothing and checked her orifices for any hidden weap-ons or tools.

Having affirmed that she wasn't carrying anything beyond what was in her backpack, one of them used her radio. "We searched her and she had nothing, save an empty skull." Iris heard Merkuroth angrily state "Oh, fuck you!" She could feel his humiliation even if she was in too much pain to do anything other than quietly whimper. "Copy that," rang Francis from the radio. "Toss her in one of the cells. I'll interrogate her later." The two women forced a metal collar of some kind on Iris, but didn't bother to put her clothes back on. They then picked her up and began carrying her down the hall.

After a few moments, they reached an area full of empty rooms. The locks were on the outside, much like one would find in a jail. Through bleary eyes, Iris looked through the windows and saw that all were empty, save one. In that, a man was doing sit-ups. He stopped, silently watching as the operators tossed her into the room and roughly tossed her clothes in after her. "Might wanna put those on if you don't want to give the men even more of a show," said one of the women before slamming the door. Iris curled up in a ball, whimpering as she stared at her bandaged stump. Her first operation had ended in utter disaster, with the only thing she had to show for it being a missing appendage and utter humiliation.

CHAPTER 7: ALEXANDER

"Iris. Can you speak?" After around an hour, the agonizing pain, both emotional and physical, subsided to the point where Iris had pulled herself up and now sat against the wall. "Yeah. Fuck. What the fuck was I thinking, getting into this? I had no idea what I was in for, I should have just stayed home," said Iris. Despondent, she could only listen as Merkuroth spoke. "You're not dead, there's likely only five enemies and you have a potential ally across from you. In your position, the first thing I'd do is make contact with him."

Though she wasn't currently curled up in a ball crying, Iris was in no condition to be making friends. She silently stared at where her left hand used to be, contemplating all the terrible decisions that lead her to this moment. Her dead father, her missing appendage, how much more would she lose before it was over? What would it being over even entail? Losing her life to this bizarre, absurd, fucked up world of supernatural powers and sociopathic pricks? She shuddered, knowing she might have gotten off lucky compared to some.

"Survey your situation. I know you're in absolutely no condition to do much right now, but you need to understand more about where you are." Wordlessly, Iris blinked until her vision cleared, then slowly pulled herself to her feet. The room had a simple cot, no windows, what appeared to be a camera dome in the upper right corner, a combined sink/toilet unit and a desk and chair. Spartan, but clearly meant for continued inhabitation. The fact that cells like this were located beneath a mansion utterly disturbed her. Given what Merkuroth had said about the formation of the cult, they were presumably built prior to them needing sacrifices. She shuddered at what some rich assholes might have done with something like this.

"Hey. Are you alright in there?" Iris heard a male voice and slowly turned towards the door, staring out the clear plexiglass window. She saw a young man, around sixteen or seventeen years of age, looking back at her with dull red eyes. His hair was a short dirty brown and he had refined Slavic features. Irritated, Iris held up her bandaged forearm in front of her. "Do I fucking look alright, asshole?" In response, he blushed and turned away. "Your, uh, clothes. Put them on, please."

After standing silently for a moment, Iris turned from the door and began dressing herself. It was extremely uncomfortable with only one hand and took her far longer than usual. After a couple minutes, she turned back towards the window and at her fellow prisoner. "Thank you. I don't, um, want to disrespect you," he said. She was astounded that that was what concerned him at the moment. "Anyway, my name is Alexander Chloraker. Can you tell me anything about what's going on here? What is this place? Who are these people?" he asked.

"Wait. Chloraker? Of the Cloraker Mining Concern?" Alexander glanced away, as though he were a bit ashamed. "Yes, the son of James Chloraker. But that's not important right now. Will you at least tell me your name?" Iris breathed, trying to steady her nerves. "Iris. Iris Kriemhild. I fucked up bad and I ended up here." Merkuroth spoke up. "Can you explain who that man is to me?" he asked. She muttered in response. "The Chloraker Mining Concern is one of the worst corporations in the Unified States of Gamma. They grew to extreme wealth and power through pretty much every horrid thing you could think of. Exploiting labor, employing strikebusters, paying off regulators. There's even rumors they outright assassinated competitors. It's a very dangerous group."

"Be on your guard, Iris. He is the enemy of your enemy, but he is no friend." Iris was irritated Merkuroth felt the need to state something so obvious. But she didn't exactly have much of a choice in who to talk to right now. Her cell didn't even have any books to read or anything to do, other than contemplate how much she hated herself right now. So, she looked back at Alexander and decided to ask a question of her own. "How did you get here?"

"Honestly, I'm not sure," said Alexander. "I got out of my limo and was walking into a hotel when someone tossed an object in front of me. I looked at it and saw a bright flash with a loud sound. A lightbanger, maybe? I hit the ground and felt something slam into the back of my head. Then I woke up in this cell with nothing but my clothes." Given how the SCA apparently tried to operate covertly, Iris doubted that they were the ones responsible for his kidnapping. She wished she had internet access right now so she could check if there were any attacks in front of hotels and verify his story.

"What do you have in there?" Iris asked. She looked around as Alexander spoke. "A bed, a toilet, a sink and a desk. Not that there's anything I could use the desk for." He trailed off, clearly dissatisfied with how long he had spent with solely those objects to keep him company. "Now answer my question. Who are those people who tossed you in?" Iris thought it best to tell the truth.

"The SCA. Supernatural Containment Agency. You know of them?" Alexander was silent for a moment. "Shitfuck. Them? They're the ones who are holding us captive? That's not good," he said. Iris replied, "No, I doubt they're the ones who kidnapped you. They were searching this place when I got here. I just stumbled into a squad of them and got my fucking hand cut off." She cringed, recalling the pain of having Francis' blade pass through her wrist. "I'm sorry to hear that," replied Alexander. "They fed me, at least. I don't know how long they're keeping us here but they clearly have plans."

"Fuck." Getting fed meant that they might have them there for quite a while. Iris wasn't one used to being alone with her own thoughts, dark as they were. She usually spent days on her computer playing games, coding and watching movies. And with her chronic insomnia, that meant she would experience even longer however she would be trapped here. She slid down against the door, burying her face in her remaining hand. Her only occupation, her only recourse, was the son of a corrupt mining magnate. "So, uh. What now?" she asked.

"Now we wait," said Alexander. "I don't think there's much else we can do. They got a mana eater collar on you, too, don't they?" Iris was confused at what he said. "A what?" she asked. "It's standard operating procedure for the SCA to put a collar on their captives. It prevents them from using magic by absorbing mana before it's channeled and shocking you if you try. I've heard some are able to overload it, though," he explained. Merkuroth spoke up. "That's intriguing. Ask him if he has any worms in there."

Iris thought that was unlikely, but asked anyway. "Got any worms in there? I might be able to do something with it." Alexander scrambled around his cell, looking for anything that could possibly qualify as one. After a few minutes, he replied, "No." The cells were lined with cold concrete so that was unlikely. That basically left them out of options. "May I try something, Iris?" asked Merkuroth. "Fine," she replied. Since she had nothing to lose, Iris gave her consent. Merkuroth took control of her body and placed her remaining hand on the concrete floor.

After a few moments, she felt the presence of worms in the dank soil. "Good, the concrete's only around a foot thick," said Merkuroth. "And the collar didn't stop my actions." Iris made an irritated expression. "You did this without knowing it would be safe?!" she exclaimed. Merkuroth replied, "If we stay within the boundaries of what we know to be safe, we won't be able to improve our situation. I hate the thought of causing you pain, but I cannot allow us to remain a captive of the SCA."

Sadly, Merkuroth was right. The only way they would be able to do anything was by taking risks. She felt a few particular worms near the sewage systems of the toilet within the dank soil beneath the concrete. "I may be able to do something with these," muttered Merkuroth. Even after all this time, the feeling of his magics was strange and unfamiliar to Iris, leading to her suppressing a shudder. Afterwards, she felt him force them to move, slowly into a crack and up the pipes. Eventually, she felt them move up through the toilet unit in Alexander's cell.

"Tell him to swallow those," said Merkuroth. Iris retched at the thought. However, given the situation they were in, she saw little alternative. "Alexander," she said. "Look in the toilet. See the worms? Swallow those." Her disgust was audible as she commanded him. "You want me to swallow worms that came from the toilet?! Are you fucking insane?" yelled Alexander. Down the hall, one of the female operators yelled, "Quiet down in there! I'm trying to read!" Alexander lowered his voice and hissed, "Why the fuck would I do that?"

"I can control worms," explained Iris. "Just do it. You want to get out of here and you know the SCA won't let you, right?" Alexander sighed in revulsion but decided to do as she said. Iris felt the worms get picked up, put into his mouth and travel down his throat. After a minute or two, Merkuroth spoke. "Good, he's proficient in the Shadow element. That makes this a lot easier." Alexander jumped, looking around his cell. "What was that?"

"A., well, friend. It's a long story." Iris really did not want to go into detail about who Merkuroth was and how she met him, but his aid would be crucial. "Can you understand him?" she asked. "No, not at all," he replied. "I just feel a strange buzzing in the back of my head, like someone's trying to talk through a defective radio." Odd explanation, thought Iris. "Good enough," said Merkuroth. "I've established a mana link. You'll be able to give him all of your mana. Hopefully that will be enough to let him overload the collar."

"You're putting a lot of faith in him, aren't you?" muttered Iris. "Yes, I am," said Merkuroth. "We have no alternative. Finally, she got up and faced him through the window again. "Tell him that when the buzzing gets really strong, that's his signal," instructed Merkuroth. "Use the strongest spell he can and keep going no matter how much it hurts." Instantly, she understood his plan. "Alexander, listen to me," said Iris. "When the buzzing is strongest, that's your moment. Cast something as hard as you can. Ignore the shocks. It might be enough to overload the collar."

"Understood," said Alexander. Iris really didn't know how much she could trust him, but for now, they were allies of convenience. They were both trapped in cells and both sought to escape. "How long will the mana link last?" asked Iris. "Around 24 hours. That's how long it will take the worms to be digested," explained Merkuroth. "If we're still trapped then, I can establish one as many times as we need. The soil has many worms, and the ability is inherent rather than dependent on mana." That sounded extremely convenient. "Are there any other inherent abilities you have?" asked Iris. "Yes," said Merkuroth, "but they are very advanced. You could not learn them at your current level, and certainly not in the state you're in."

That just left them to wait for some form of opportunity. Iris doubted they would be kept in these cells forever. What if she helped him to escape and he simply abandoned her? What if they simply decided to execute them? What if they were transported to a more secure prison with no such opportunities, abilities like Merkuroth's planned and accounted for? She shuddered at the possibility. Not knowing what was going to happen to her was the worst part of her experience.

"What magics can you use?" asked Iris. Alexander took a moment to answer. "I don't think we should talk about that now," he said.

"And it's rather personal." He was certainly cagey on that front, which made Iris suspect he had a lot to hide. "Merkuroth, what can you tell?" she muttered. Similarly, the demon also took a moment to reply. "Not much," he said. "His magic circuits are of great quality but average quantity. He seems the sort to use typical spells in creative ways." It sounded a lot like he spoke from experience.

So, Iris thought it best to rest. There wasn't much more to talk about with Alexander if he was going to be uncommunicative about his abilities. That made it difficult for them to formulate further plans. It was difficult, being forced to trust in a disreputable stranger. Her missing hand hurt. She remembered the phenomena of phantom limb pains, the agony of a body part that was no longer there. It was surreal to her to still feel the pain of losing something she had all her life.

Iris lay in her bed, closing her eyes and willing her mind to rest. It was never something she was good at, always playing out scenarios, recalling past events and formulating new actions she could take. Perhaps that was why she was such an insomniac. Eventually, however, she gradually drifted into unconsciousness, her sleep fitful and disturbed.

With the bang of her meal tray slot being opened and having something shoved through, Iris awakened. Immediately, she remembered her missing hand. She supposed these pangs of agony at missing a body part would be with her for quite some time. How was she going to function without it? "Merkuroth," she muttered, "Is there anything I can do about my hand?"

"Given enough time and resources, yes," Merkuroth explained. "You can learn the Life discipline of magic and gradually regrow it. This will take a while and a lot of effort, but for a mage, no injury need be permanent." Gradually, she forced herself to a sitting position and looked through her cell's window. "Hey, Alexander," she asked, "How long has it been since I laid down?" She saw him speaking with his mouth full of food. "Uhh, a couple hours, I think?"

That was longer than Iris could usually sleep. She looked down at her meal and saw a sandwich, a cup of water and some beans. Hardly anything worth getting excited for, but she had no choice but to take what she could get. Eating with one hand was awkward and unfamiliar, but she managed. Soon she finished her meager meal and put the tray in a corner. With no other tools, perhaps it would prove useful somehow.

CHAPTER 8: INTERROGATION

Iris spent a few hours in silence, lamenting her circumstances. Something had to change eventually. It just had to. They wouldn't keep her here forever. As it turned out, she was right. Eventually, the two female SCA operators who had searched her earlier came to her cell door and opened it. "Lieutenant wants to speak with you. Come with us." With one hand, no magic and no weapons, Iris was in no position to resist. She pulled herself to her feet and walked out of the cell, sparing a glance to Alexander. Once more, he was doing situps in his cell. The woman behind Iris shoved her forward.

One operator stood in front of her and one behind. They were obviously trained in dealing with potentially dangerous captives this way. Iris had no escape so she simply walked forward, following the one in front's lead. All three of them proceeded down the hallway and eventually reached another door. It was opened by the woman in front and the one behind her unceremoniously shoved her inside before both filed in. Inside was Francis Sullivan, sitting on a cheap metal chair at the end of the table. In front of him was a briefcase and an ice box labeled CHAD MCCOOL.

"Sit," Francis commanded. Iris knew better than to refuse, so she sat on another cheap metal chair at the other end of the table. He opened the briefcase in front of him and tossed a few documents in front of Iris. She spotted her name and portrait, as well as a few personal details, but didn't bother to leaf through them. So, he spoke.

"Iris Kriemhild, age 15. Sex F, blood type AB negative. Net worth $30,000, primarily funded through the coding and sale of several stalkerware apps. Widely used among controlling spouses and overprotective parents. Don't you think making those was kind of a dick move? You're clearly capable of better things," he admonished her. Francis leaned back and laced his fingers behind his head. "What the fuck is this?" spat Iris. "Some sort of morality tale? Asshole." Merkuroth chimed in. "Do not allow him to upset you, Iris. It's a standard interrogation tactic. Do you wish me to take over?" Subtly, she shook her head and stared back at Francis. He continued.

"Graduated high school online at 12, no formal employment since then. Guess you're too good for that. Lived with parents until age 13, when the disappearance of your mother left you living with a single father. You clearly loved him, though, given that you could have easily gone elsewhere," he chided her. "Smart kids like you often do that" Francis' goading was incredibly obvious. This time, she just silently stared at him, waiting for anything else. After a few moments, he went on.

"Now, here's the part I find interesting. You go to a theme park with your father where he also disappears without a trace. You just go home and say that's all you know when my partner and I came to interrogate you," said Francis. Iris interjected. "Your partner's a homophobic dick." He laughed. "Yes, yes he is. Not much I can do about that, though. But anyway. You refuse entry and we can't force the way. We go away to investigate why your father disappeared. You just so happen to show up where we were investigating with lockpicks, hacking tools and scariest of all, a baseball bat with nails through it."

Iris clenched her fist, angered by Francis' observations and deduction. Merkuroth spoke to soothe her. "No. Not yet. Wait until they're furthest into it." The SCA Lieutenant continued. "Now, how would you know anything about the cult that abducted your father? Option one, you were there and found something leading you here. I find that extremely unlikely given that the person we nearly apprehended at the scene didn't have enough time and likely not enough knowledge to find anything useful." She shuddered, knowing how she had just barely escaped back then with the aid of Merkuroth.

"Option two," Francis spoke.

"You're a demonhost, aren't you?"

Iris' eyes widened at his deduction, causing him to laugh. "I knew it! God, I bet that demon is so pissed now!" Not only was she shocked at his deduction, but scared of what Merkuroth was thinking. "But here's the truth," he continued. "I had some help in finding out just what you were." He reached into his briefcase and this time took out a small binder and set it in front of her. Shaking, she opened it, finding an enumerated list within.

Contents of safe found within Hans Kriemhild's room:

1. $5000 cash
2. Armko-19 pistol, 9 rounds in magazine
3. Handwritten note, contents enumerated below
4. Dragon necklace, Magicore embedded within
5. Flash drive containing financial and legal documents

With her remaining hand, Iris leafed through the binder and found images of all the things enumerated in the list. She had these in her house the whole time? Owning a firearm was a very serious crime and she had one within her home. Eventually, she came upon a handwritten note, wrinkled but well-preserved, and pulled it out. "Ooh, this is the good part," said Francis. "Read it!" Shaking, she looked it over.

To my beautiful Iris,

If you're reading this, I've failed to protect you. I left it knowing you would be able to break into this safe and find what was within. Please, use everything here to protect yourself from the dangers you are certain to face.

I am sorry to say I have become a murderer and deprived you of your mother in the hopes you would not follow in her footsteps. She sought to teach you of the dangerous, forbidden world of magic, exposing you to horrors I would never want you to experience. I couldn't allow this, but she allowed no reproach. There was nothing I could do, but I simply could not accept you being drawn into a world where cruelty is compulsory and human lives are merely a resource to be exploited. So, I took her life in order to ensure your safety in ignorance.

I can only hope that your intelligence, your resourcefulness, your resources and your cunning can help you in a way I could not. I would have given anything to live just one day longer than the daughter I loved, but I failed. I am so sorry. Do whatever you must to survive.

Red Tail 9

Hans Kriemhild

Iris looked up from the note at Francis with waving eyes. In a few seconds, tears began streaming down her face. "What the fuck?" she asked. Red Tail 9 was their secret passcode, known only to them. Hans often reminded her of it, ensuring she knew it meant something directly from him. She knew it was her father by those words. Not only had she lost her father, he had deprived her of her mother. She laid her head on the table, barely comprehending what she had just read.

"Iris," said Francis. "You have a choice here. You can become a victim to circumstance, a slave of that demon and never knowing what you're truly capable of." She felt static buzzing loudly at the back of her head as her mana was drained. It was a strange sensation, like urinating but leaving her extremely fatigued. "Or, you can join us. We pay you a shitload and you'll get anything you need. That demon taken out? Done. Newest tech out there? You got it. If you agree to help us, to become one of us, I'll attach your hand right now." She lifted her head and saw him open the ice box. Her severed hand, preserved by strange crystals emanating cold, lay within.

"Or we could give you some badass augment instead. Whatever you prefer. You know what they say, turn a setback into an opportunity!" shouted Francis. Iris was infuriated by his cavalier attitude and seeming disregard for everything she went through. He treated everything like a joke and had zero compassion for her losses and her suffering. "Your pitch is asinine," said Iris. "You offer me material wealth to work for you and do to others what you've done to me. That's not something I'll ever do." It was perhaps the first bit of confidence she had shown against him, and it was extremely satisfying.

"Well, that's unfortunate. Here's the bad news. If you don't agree to this, you'll be transported to a much, much more secure prison," said Francis. "I can't say what will happen to you. Perhaps you'll be experimented on, perhaps they'll just hold onto you until you agree. It's not up to me. But the truth is, Iris, I like you a lot. I think you're capable of becoming an extremely competent officer. Thus far, you've shown intelligence, daring, creativity and-" The door creaked as it was opened and Alexander stepped inside.

He rushed forward, slamming into one of the female soldiers and jamming a piece of metal into her throat. She gurgled and collapsed as she choked on her own blood. Alexander then proceeded to yank her pistol from its holster and fire three rounds at the other operator, two impacting her body armor and the third penetrating her face. Francis yelled, "FUCK!" as he drew his katana, waving it in front of him as Alexander emptied the magazine at him.

Afterwards, Francis stood unharmed, staring with wide eyes at Alexander tossed his pistol aside and assumed a martial arts stance. Concrete from the floor rose up, coating his fists and forearms. Iris clutched her head on the floor, disoriented by the loud noises of the firearm in a confined space. Her vision swam, her head rang, she felt like puking from the cacophony.

"Bastard!" yelled Francis. Then, he stepped forward, his katana once more coated in blue and yellow light flecks. Faster than should be humanly possible, he swung at Alexander in trained, precise blows. However, he was met in kind by his concrete-coated fists. Slowly, they got chipped away, leaving his arms bare.

"Iris. Move." Still feeling nauseous, she got up, looking around for a weapon. The second woman he killed still had a pistol in her holster. She crawled forward, grabbing it in her remaining hand and aiming it at Francis. It was extremely difficult to aim, as she had never used a firearm in her life and the two of them danced around the table, looking for any opening.

Merkuroth took control, and with much more precision, fired at Francis' ankles. It passed through his tibia, causing him to collapse and hit the floor. He continued firing, the rounds impacting his body armor but failing to penetrate. As he groaned in pain, Alexander walked forward and slammed his head into the concrete floor repeatedly. Eventually, he lay still and silent, his skull caved in and blood pooled around him. So, he picked up one of the operator's rifles and slung it across his shoulder, then grabbed Francis' katana from his silent body. He then tied the cord to his own waist, preparing it for use if necessary.

"Sorry about that. Thought it best to do an ambush." Iris was unable to hear him or accept his hand as her head swam from the unsuppressed gunfire. She threw up and clutched her head, extreme disorientation and nausea overtaking her. It took her a couple minutes to recover before she could speak and hear again. Alexander grabbed Francis' radio before he silently stood guard, watching for any further interlopers. Eventually, she rose to her feet. "You... You just killed three people!" she yelled. "No. I killed five,"Alexander corrected her. "Two I incinerated, one I jabbed a knife made from my tray into her throat, one I shot, one whose skull I bashed in. But that is irrelevant. We need to move!"

"He is right, Iris." said Merkuroth. "You can consider the morality of his actions later. You need to escape before more of them show up." Grabbing the CHAD MCCOOL ice box, Iris ran forward, following Alexander as he went up the stairs, the single entrance of the prison beneath the mansion. "You know the way?" Iris asked. "Not at all," said Alexander, "But it is best we are not here when they are coming!"

Iris thought over where she had been and spoke up. "Take a left here, then a right three doors down." They ran forward, down the corridors and towards the front entrance. The ice box containing her right hand painfully bounced against her left, but she had no choice but to continue onward. After a while, they eventually reached the front entrance, where Iris had first entered the mansion.

"Know anything about where we are?" asked Alexander. "Uhh, yeah, 1770 Broadson Avenue. One of those isolated compounds you see rich families construct," replied Iris. "I got here from a bike... shit." Iris swore to herself as they emerged into the afternoon sunlight. "What the fuck do we do now?" she asked.

Alexander was silent for a moment. Merkuroth spoke to Iris. "Consider your apartment lost. They already raided it and they will have it under surveillance." Iris shuddered at the realization that all of her material possessions, everything that was once her father's, all of the games she had once played, all of the online friends she once had, all of the media library she had painstakingly curated for herself and her father - all of that was gone now. Now she was left with nothing, save her clothes, her bike and the man standing beside her.

Unaware of her turmoil, Alexander spoke up. "I have one of these rich people compounds a few dozen miles away. Getting there will be difficult at best. How did you get to this mansion?" he asked. With a grimace, Iris explained, "I biked. " He also grimaced, fully aware of the precariousness of their situation. "Show me," he said.

Locked to a bush, for both concealment and security, was her bike. She lifted it up and pulled it out, but the chain held it back. "Motherfucker, no key!" swore Iris. The women had taken it from her when they searched her. Silently, Alexander reached out and gripped the chain. After a moment, he released it and two separate ends fell apart. "I'm nearly out of mana, but I can do this much," he explained.

Alexander then pulled out the bike and examined it. Once more, he used magic to separate the basket from the back and tossed it into the woods. "Can you use Fire magic?" he asked. "No," answered Iris. "Just Shadow." Alexander swore, "Shit. Setting a fire would help to cover our tracks and inhibit pursuit, but I just don't have the mana for that." With that, he mounted the bicycle and told her, "Get on the back. It's our only option other than walking."

Iris realized that there was no space for the CHAD MCCOOL ice box. "But my hand," she whimpered. Alexander had a look of pain as he explained, "We don't exactly have a choice. There's no room for both you and the basket. I promise you, I'll do everything I can to get you a superior prosthetic. But for now, we need to move."

With the basket gone, there was just enough room for the two of them. Morosely, Iris rode side-saddle on the rack, balancing herself by putting her remaining hand on Alexander's shoulder. It was quite difficult for her, both because she wasn't used to balancing that way and because she disliked physical contact. As the bike was an electric model, it was nearly silent as the two of them sped off away from the mansion.

CHAPTER 9: HIDEOUT

They were both out of mana, making them exhausted and unable to use magic. One of them was missing a hand and the other was doing his best to protect her. Iris assumed that the squad hadn't been able to get an alert off to the larger SCA organization before Alexander killed all five of them. She cringed at the realization that she was holding onto someone who was not only able, but willing to kill five trained operators.

"Uh, what about the rifle and katana?" asked Iris. The former painfully jabbed into her front as they sped through alleys, back roads and a construction site, trying to keep out of sight. "What of them?" asked Alexander. "Don't they make us look suspicious?" Alexander went quiet for a bit. "Shit. Yes, it does, but if we ditch it, we'll be even more defenseless and leaving something behind might help them track us. I have no weapons in my safehouse, so it's best we have something to help us."

The situation looked worse and worse as time went on. For a while, they let the electric motor do the work, Alexander merely steering its direction. Iris looked around as best she could, but she couldn't see behind her. There was no sign of pursuing SCA forces and the worst they got were some odd looks. Witnesses, perhaps. Not the best thing to leave behind, but they had no choice.

What was next? Eventually they came upon it. Alexander stopped the bike and held his hand out in front of him. "Here we are," he said. Iris dismounted, looking it over. It was a normal, unassuming lower-middle class rental home in the middle of a plethora of others. Hiding in plain sight kept them safe. It wasn't too dissimilar from her old apartment.

"Why do you even have something like this?" asked Iris. "Safety," he answered. "Safety? What do you mean?" Alexander took a moment to reply. "Many reasons. Say there's a working class revolution against my father's company. I'll need a safe, unassuming place to stay if I don't want to be targeted. Say my father is stripped of all assets through legal means. I own this house, so I will be unaffected. Say my father disowns me for my activities. I have many homes in different places."

They dismounted the bike and Alexander walked to the front door. A quick jiggle yielded no results. "Damn. Locked," he muttered. Iris spoke up. "I can pick locks. We'll just go to the back and... shit." Once more, she realized she was deprived of her abilities due to her missing hand. "What are we going to do now?" she asked.

"Hmm." Alexander began testing the windows. They were all locked, barring the pair's entrance. They proceeded to the back window only to find similar results. "I don't think we have any options other than breaking a window. Iris, do you have any ideas?" It was something Iris wished to avoid, given that they wanted to evade the SCA and it would look rather suspicious. "Shit, um." She reviewed her options. There was no chimney to climb into. She couldn't pick locks with only one hand and Alexander couldn't be taught so quickly. Her kit was stolen by the guards, anyway. They were both out of mana so that wasn't an option. "Yeah. No choice."

"Well, then." Alexander picked up a nearby stone and bashed in a window. Iris cringed at the noise, hoping no one would react. The walls in the backyard prevented anyone from seeing their break-in. He reached through, undid the latch and slid it open. "Can you climb in? You're smaller than I am." She blushed at the frank assessment.

Alexander gave her a boost and Iris climbed through the window.

As expected, it was a modest rental home with four rooms. No furniture was inside it, leaving her a lot of room to maneuver. She stumbled and fell through the window, leaving her with a miner gash on her leg from broken glass. With a grunt of pain, she slowly rose to her feet. No glass was left in her wound, thankfully, nor were any arteries nicked. Still, she'd need some medical attention.

Iris walked out of the living room and unlocked the front door. After a minute, Alexander came in and wheeled the bike through. He parked it in the living room before walking back to the front door, locking it again. "You seriously didn't stock any furniture, appliances, or anything that might have helped us? Really?" she asked. "You need to understand, Iris," replied Alexander. "I have many things to take care of. Getting kidnapped, tossed into a cell, being left for a few days before being discovered by the SCA wasn't among my priorities."

With a sigh, Iris sat down against the wall. She stared at her bandaged forearm, thinking over her situation. "Well, what do we do? We have nothing. No phone, no computer, no couch to rest on, not even a fucking microwave to make some food. I'm starving," she complained. Alexander sat next to her. She cringed at how close he was. He spoke. "I have a few secret accounts. Tell me what you need and I'll run out and get it."

Alexander planned to leave her here? Iris was deeply uncomfortable with the prospect. But she would do nothing but slow him down, and hopefully, the SCA wouldn't be able to find them in a safehouse like this. "Um. Get me a laptop. A place to sleep. And where's that prosthetic hand you promised? And a pizza." There are no problems in life that cannot be mitigated with pizza, she mused. "Alright. I'll ensure you have everything you need, but it will take time. I promise you, Iris, I will do everything in my power to protect you," said Alexander.

It was suspicious how he was being so helpful to someone who he just met. He could have abandoned her several times over but he refused. "Why are you so nice to me?" she asked. Even when she cringed at his touch or his sitting close to her, he remained as kind as he could be. "Because, Iris, you helped me escape. I owe you a lot for that. The SCA and the Chloraker Mining Concern are not on good terms." He went in for a hug and Iris scuttled back.

"Don't touch me, please," Iris muttered. "Uh, sorry." replied Alexander. "I'll be back soon. I can't do a lot right now, but I will help you. For now, I'm leaving the weapons." With that, he set down the katana and rifle before taking the bike and walked toward the front door. After unlocking it, he went through the entrance and closed it behind him. Once again, she was left alone. She sighed before laying down on the carpeted floor. "Merkuroth, are you there?" she asked.

"I am always here," the demon replied. Strangely, his grating, gravelly voice was becoming more familiar and less terrifying to her. So, she asked "What do I do now?"

"Right now, I don't believe you have much of an option other than to trust Alexander. But if he betrays you, it would be best if you had an exit plan." Iris reviewed her surroundings. All she could do is run out the back door and into the alleyways again. With no mana, she wouldn't have much of a chance. Even so, in an urban environment, many things can be used. Even hiding in a dumpster can help keep you safe from enemies.

It was awful how used to this she was getting. She'd already lost so much to the world of magic - her father, her hand, her possessions, her status as an unwanted citizen rather than a fugitive. Undoubtedly, the SCA would freeze all of her assets, confiscate everything of hers they could find and set up alarms if she attempted to access anything.. At least, anything they knew about. She made plans for later, to reclaim certain possessions she hid from their view. With proper cryptography and discretion, anything can be hidden.

Iris took off her hoodie and folded it into a crude pillow before laying down on it. She was exhausted and thought she might as well take a quick nap while she had the time. At least, if she could, anyway. Her sleep was fitful and restless even before all of this happened, when she thought the world was cruel but rational. But oddly enough, she seemed to have learned to sleep as much as she could when she could.

I stared forward at the enemy before me, clearly an experienced Sylvani operative. She wielded light leather armor, made from mythic beasts of some kind. In her right hand was a mystic saber, in her left, the powerful light of magefire. I clearly faced an experienced opponent, ready and willing to kill me. I feared no armies, nor any leaders. Not since I killed the First. But individual champions provided a greater challenge than any.

I spoke. "None shall stand before the salvation of Man." Even muttering, I knew her Sylvani ears would be able to hear it. "Aeryikas. She is yours."

My hellhound shivered at the opportunity, slowly emerging from the southwest. I stared onward, prepared to watch the ensuing battle. Aeryikas was my beloved companion, the sole recompense for my brutal experiment which resulted in my parent's death. But in the face of my goals, he was expendable. Everything was expendable, even my dear brother.

The woman flipped her saber into a reverse grip and twisted, jabbing towards my hellhound. She spared only a glance, verifying that her saber had hit its mark, before turning back to me. Aeryikas' vertical mouth opened, a screech of pain escaping a punctured throat, before the saber alighted with magefire. Chunks of Fel-tainted flesh flew through the air, the woman protecting herself from its corrosive effects with calculated bursts of magefire.

Aeryikas' body dissolved into purplish-black smoke, floating back towards my body. She flicked her saber, sending green blood flying to the ground.

"Fencer. Sylvani. You stand before the salvation of Man." I spoke again. I walked closer. I stared at her through my mask's plexiglass eyes. She shivered in fear, gripping her blade for reassurance against my Fel power. In spite of her abject terror, she stood firm, prepared to fight. I admired her courage.

I drew my sword, a simple two feet of steel. It was nothing compared to hers, but the true value of a weapon is the skill of the wielder. I extended my right hand, cloaking it in Fel dark green fire. Her tactics required I remain able to counter her own magics.

"Fetid demonspawn!" she shouted, her voice steady in spite of her horror. "You are no salvation! You are a blight to this world, slaughtering innocents and the wicked alike! This goes no further!" Another hero sent to kill me. Their determination was commendable.

I widened my eyes and ran toward her. Once more, she waited for the right moment. I extended my right hand, cloaked in Fel fire. In an instant, she adjusted her stance, shifting her blade into her left hand and twisting, slashing at my magic-covered hand.

The blade hit its mark.

The blade sunk into my flesh.

The Fel fire harmlessly discharged past her body as she regained her footing.

The blade fractured, unable to cope with the Fel energies coursing through it from my body. Reduced to dust, it harmlessly drifted lazily onto the ground. Holding only a hilt, the Sylvani fencer widened her eyes in shock.

I took advantage of her astonishment in order to end the battle. I thrust my own blade forward towards her chest. She jumped backwards, a poorly executed maneuver but one that saved her life. She fell and scrambled backwards in an attempt to buy enough time to get back on her feet.

"Surrender, Sylvani. You will aid the salvation of Man and you will be remembered," I said. She was left defenseless. No weapon remained to stop me in my quest to attain peace and harmony for the world.

The Sylvani lifted her legs then flung them forward. Her impressive abdominal strength allowed her to easily jump to her feat. She had no weapon. So, she raised her fists, switching to unarmed combat in order to overcome me. Her right hand joined her left, cloaked in magefire ready to be used against me.

I moved in for a diagonal slash, thinking I had the advantage. She jumped to the left, grabbing my wrist and discharging her magefire into my body. My arm exploded, scattering more chunks of Fel-tainted gore across the cracked streets. Ignoring the pain, I shot my left hand towards her chest. She reacted, but far too late.

It burned away her light leather armor, her flesh, her ribcage, then her heart, imploded by my Fel magics. Her heart imploded. She went limp. In respect for her efforts, I spoke. "Brave. You will be remembered."

Iris awoke with a cold sweat covering her in spite of the moderate temperature. "What the fuck?!" she yelled, the vivid nightmare shaking her to her core. She bolted upwards, then onto her feet, looking around herself. She was still in the abandoned home Alexander brought her to. However, there was no sign of him, only a faint outline on the floor from her perspiration.

"Are you alright, Iris?" asked Merkuroth. Iris sat down against the wall, idly playing with the slightly damp carpet. "Yeah, I just had a really awful nightmare," she explained. "It was so vivid."

"Oh?" Intrigued, Merkuroth pressed further. "What happened?"

"Well, uh, I was this really powerful demon thing who wanted to kill a bunch of people, I guess. And there was this woman with pointed ears who stood against me," she recounted. "Despite her being my enemy, I admired her a lot. Like she was some kind of hero." Merkuroth was silent. Iris sat there, still poking her finger at the carpet. Eventually, he spoke. "What you're experiencing, Iris, are my memories."

Horrified, Iris jumped to her feet. "Your memories? You did something like that in life?" The familiar disgust with the demon from their first days together returned. She realized that her suspicions about him being a foreign entity with alien values were never disproven. He simply didn't intend to harm her. Merkuroth continued speaking. "I told you when we first met. I needed to accomplish a significant goal which required a great sacrifice. Some simply thought it was worth defending the lives of those needed above achieving that goal."

Iris buried her face in her hands, once more forced to confront just who was within her. She was sharing a body with a mass murderer who was both able and willing to kill anyone who would try to stop him. At least, that's what he did in his own life, in another world and long since past. What would she do knowing who she was forced to cooperate with?

"How many have you killed?" Iris choked out. Once more, he was silent. Then, the demon spoke quietly. "Tens of thousands. Logistically, keeping track was difficult, but the magics I harvested from them through various means were approximate to that number." She gasped at the quantity. She had expected a few hundred at most, but that was a forlorn hope. But that still left a single question; why? What goal could possibly justify killing so many people?

"What did you hope to accomplish in the end?" asked Iris. Seemingly prepared for this question, Merkuroth spoke. "My world was consumed with strife of all kinds. Conflicts raged endlessly across everywhere I went, leading to constant suffering. Refugee crises, pillaging, extreme poverty. I had witnessed enough to conclude that a radical solution was necessary. I was, however, fortunate enough to be born with 80 magic circuits and a comfortable enough lifestyle to develop my abilities."

"My brother was utterly uninterested. I attempted, on many occasions, to convince him that it was our role to improve society. Being given the means and the comprehension of its flaws made us obligated to solve the problems presented to us. He was utterly uninterested in anything other than deepening his own knowledge and power. So, on my own, I attempted to gain enough to forge a new order. At first, I succeeded, learning many new magics and techniques. But one night, I attempted a dangerous summoning of a demon."

Iris grimaced, living with the consequences of a cult which attempted to do something very similar. Merkuroth continued. "I failed. My parents investigated and I lost control. The Felfire incinerated them. My brother barely survived. Many dark energies were discharged into me, tainting my body and eventually my very essence. I was no longer a son of both human and Sylvani, I was something entirely different. From there, we fled, seeking out our own objectives. He stood against me and failed. A cult I had used created thirteen extremely powerful beings. I had killed several, but I eventually fell to one which stood against me in spite of its betrayal of that cult."

"So now you understand, Iris." She did, though the explanation was far from what she hoped it would be. "What is your next objective? If you seek to be free of me, I will aid you. If you seek to destroy me, I will aid you. I failed. You will not," said Merkuroth. The nature of a mass murdering demon was now clear to her. Formerly mortal, he embodied the worst aspects of sapient life, seeking destruction, death, all to achieve what he sought to impose upon society. And above all, he promised her his aid.

"Fuck." Iris couldn't say anything more than that. Nausea gripped her. If her stomach were not empty already she would have voided it. "I think I hate you," she muttered. "Oh, that is very understandable," said Merkuroth. "I never thought I was a very good person. Or demon, in my case."

For a few minutes, she sat in silence, thinking over everything she had learned. "I don't want this to happen again. To anyone," she affirmed to herself. Soon after, there was a knock on the door. Alexander walked in, with a newly filled backpack and Iris' electric bike. "Hey," he said. "You alright? Sorry to leave you for so long."

"How long has it been?" Iris asked. "A few hours," Alexander explained. "Here, let's set everything up." He set down his new backpack and unzipped it before beginning to unload it. There was the standard assortment of basic survival gear, pocket knives, map and compass, mylar blankets, notepads, pencils, lighters. If their situation got worse, they would have the bare minimum to survive. For provisions, he had some other goods, granola bars, freeze-dried meals, a saucepan to boil water in, protein powder. It would be enough to hide out in this house for at least a week.

"I got some money and visited a camping store. Other than that, I also got us some prepaid phones and a laptop," said Alexander. He handed both to Iris. She stared at them for a moment. "Fruit-Berries and a Targa 19? Seriously?" She was mystified as to how he could be so ignorant to both of their negative reputations. Shortly afterward, she realized she was being pretty selfish. "Hey, I don't know a lot about computers," he said. "I was hoping you could teach me a couple things. For now, can you set them up?"

"Yeah, sorry. It's just stressful," Iris apologized, beginning to boot them all up. She exchanged their contact info and set them aside for the moment. Afterwards, she started visiting obscure darknet websites to go about the process of disabling any and all tracking. "What are you doing?" asked Alexander, utterly mystified. He stared with rapt attention as she accessed servers he had never even heard of before. "Well, the SCA's listening, right? I don't want them starting to look around and figuring out we have some convenient trackers right on us."

"Oh. Yes, it is very good that you will be teaching me these things," said Alexander. His admiration was audible. Iris continued. After around an hour, he handed one of the phones to him. "Now we can keep in contact without worrying about anyone listening. That said, we're going to swap these out weekly. For that matter, we probably shouldn't stay in one place too long." said Iris.

"Yes, I have many homes we can go to. I'll hear if one of them gets raided," explained Alexander. "How? How will you hear? We need to think about specifics here. For that instance, how did you get the money?" questioned Iris. "Oh, dead drops. I stashed some in various places in case something like this ever happened," he said. Seemingly realizing something, he reached into the backpack once more and handed her a few bundles of money. "Here, if you need anything."

Iris' eyes bulged at the amount. While her efforts developing stalkerware had certainly not left her destitute, seeing this much cash in person was astonishing to her. "Holy crap. And you just left this lying around?" she asked. "Well, uh, I don't know much about computers. Do you know of a safer way?" he asked.

"As a matter of fact, I do." Once more, Iris got to work on the laptop. "I have a few Ripcoin wallets stashed on a couple remote servers. I can just access those, decrypt them and we have access to untraceable digital funds." It didn't take long for her to do that, and now the duo had both physical and electronic resources. "What is this Ripcoin?" asked Alexander. "Well, uh." Iris took around a minute to come up with layman's terms. "Basically, it's a digital form of money, can't be traced, can't be counterfeited, that people often use when they need to keep things anonymous."

"There's just one thing I need to know, Alex." Iris took a deep breath. Asking this wasn't going to be easy and she feared what the answer might be. "Why are you helping me so much? Why are you willing to work with me? You're some rich kid and I'm a computer geek nobody. You seem like you could easily cut a deal with the SCA and get off scot-free. Worst case scenario, you disavow your father, since you said the Chlorakers and the SCA don't get along."

Alexander also took a breath before he explained. "I've seen people pushed around by powers bigger than them all my life. At least, ever since I decided to stop being ignorant to it. I couldn't simply stand in that cell while it happened again and a weak young woman was taken advantage of." Iris turned bright red at what he said. "I know. I'm a fugitive, but I knew this would happen at some point in my life. As for my father, he's a horrible person but I love him. I don't want to cut contact with him. Not permanently, anyway."

"Be careful, Iris," interjected Merkuroth. "You don't know if you can trust his words."

The demon was right. But Iris had little alternative. On her own, it would only be a matter of time until she was caught by the SCA. She spoke. "So, uh, here's what we need. First off, my hand. You told me you'd get me a prosthetic and I'm holding you to that. Second off, I got some pizzas on the way since I'm starving and want to eat something good. Third off, I ordered some computer hardware we'll need. We'll pick it up at a nearby Amazo locker since I'd rather not have deliveries coming here."

"Wait, you'd rather not have deliveries coming here? Then why did you order a pizza?" asked Alexander, confused.

"Fuck. Well, whatever, we'll just hope no one notices." Iris was irritated with herself for her lapse in judgment, but quickly realized she was in a rough spot either way. Alexander goes out, he risks getting nabbed. They order things, they risk the neighbors catching on to them living there. When possible, the latter seemed like a better state of affairs given that the SCA likely wasn't going to give up their manhunt anytime soon.

Their manhunt would likely eventually lead to Alexander's assets being traced. Which meant that his houses might be searched. Their situation was very precarious. They would need to keep moving. "So, tell me about your magics, Alexander," said Iris. He was reluctant but eventually relented. "Fine. I'm Fire/Earth/Death/Shadow/Space, with 45 magic circuits. You know what that means, right?" he said. Iris nodded. "I'm best at Fire and Earth. What about you?"

"Just Shadow," said Iris. "But I'm really, really fuckin' good at it. Once we eat the pizza, I'll show you a few things. Think you might be able to do the same?" A knock on the door interrupted their conversation. Alexander got up to answer it. She heard the delivery guy yell "Holy shit, dude, thank you so much!" and soon Alexander walked to the living room holding five pizza boxes in one hand and two soda bottles in the other. Strangely, he seemed not to have any trouble carrying the massive amount of food. "Think you got enough food, Iris? We might starve at this rate," he chided her.

"Why was he so astonished?" asked Iris. "I gave him a $100 tip," said Alexander. Iris leaned her head back in exasperation. "Alex, you realize we're trying to avoid attention here, right?" He began setting up the food for the both of them. It was a very welcome provision, given what they had been through. "Sorry. I should have thought that through better," he apologized.

They voraciously devoured their food and chugged their soda. Restraint meant nothing to them, as their bodies needed great sustenance. The bodies of magi needed many calories to function properly. Eventually, they finished their meal, set aside what little they hadn't consumed for later, and resumed their conversation. "I promised to show you a couple things. First off is this." Iris climbed to her feet and extended her left hand. It became cloaked in smoky shadows which rapidly encompassed her entire body.

Alexander looked astonished. "It seems very useful for an infiltration mission!" he said, staring at rapt attention. "Anything else you can do?" In response to that, Iris retracted the shadows into her hand, compressing it and forming it into a bust of a middle-aged man. Though no color could be discerned from the bizarre sculpture, the resemblance between him and Iris was obvious. Their facial features had many similarities as well as their slightly curly hair. "My father," said Iris. "Hans Kriemhild. I loved him and I miss him."

"Did something happen to him?" asked Alexander. "Yeah. He got sacrificed to summon a demon," explained Iris. "It's how I got introduced to the SCA." Alexander was quiet. "I'm sorry. Losing family is painful, especially for a fucking demon," he said. Iris leaned in, intrigued. "You have experience with demons?" she asked.

"Yeah, some," he explained. "My father experimented a bit with them in his endless quest for more power. His only real success was getting his kid, born with magic circuits, the Shadow attribute. You're far more skilled with it than I am, though."

Iris glanced outside the window and saw the evening sky through the cracks of the curtains. "It's getting late. Let's rest for a while." They each took what they needed for sleeping and went into separate rooms. It didn't take long to set up a rudimentary sleeping position and with that, she easily drifted off to sleep, exhausted from their flight.

The next morning, Iris woke up and went to the living room to find Alexander shirtless and doing pushups. She watched as sweat glistened and fell down his well-toned body, gathering and dripping onto the rug. After finishing his set, he rolled over and looked at her. "Damn, you're ripped," she said.

"Um. Thanks." Alexander had a minor blush as Iris looked over his chiseled physique. He clearly took physical training extremely seriously if he was this dedicated to it. She knelt down next to him and spoke. "Want me to heat up the pizza from last night? Wait, shit, no microwave. Guess we're eating it cold." She watched in silence as he finished up his morning workout and they sat together eating cold three meat pizza.

"You know, we really could have gotten some folding camping chairs," said Iris. "Problem is, if we're moving around, that's one more thing to carry," explained Alexander. He was right. Iris resolved to think more about the problem of comfortable seating when they could transport so little.

"So what now?" asked Iris. "We have an entire day and I doubt you want to spend it watching movies." With no delay, Alexander said, "Today we get your new hand!" Iris smiled at the thought of regaining the functionality she lost to Francis' blade. The katana lay next to them and though she had mixed feelings about it, she knew weaponry could prove essential to their survival. "Get ready. I'm taking a shower." Iris longingly watched Alexander's back as he walked to the bathroom.

"What do you think, Merkuroth?" she asked. He had no hesitation in replying, "I think you need to learn to deal with your sexual attraction in a way that doesn't compromise your safety." Iris felt her face flash a hot red, before she replied, "Like you've never been into someone you're close to!"

By way of response, Merkuroth calmly stated, "As a matter of fact, I haven't. At 16, I lost my external reproductive organs and began running my body off of magical energy to the greatest extent possible. And before that, I wasn't very well liked by the other children. My brother was more the socialite, in spite of his amoral goals." If Iris' demon was willing to call someone else amoral, she knew that he must have been a truly terrifying person. "What was his name?" she asked.

"Arkuroth."

Alexander, now fully clothed, walked down the hallway and to Iris. "Ready?" She nodded. "Let's go." They grabbed the bike and precariously balanced on it again, this time setting out towards an entirely new destination. Unfortunately, they had to leave the rifle and katana behind, as there simply was no way to inconspicuously carry them. The pair had taken enough risks simply bringing it with them when they fled from the mansion.

"So, where are we going?" asked Iris. "A friend of mine has a lab," said Alexander. "He won't mess with anything magical, but we can at least get you a hand." It was a good thing, too, since Iris was sorely missing her dominant hand. The trip there was fairly uneventful, with the pair sharing a meaningless conversation about the pizza and their temporary home. After around a half hour, they arrived at their destination, a tall corporate building with security at the front desk.

Alexander produced a badge from somewhere and presented it. Dull and uninterested, the guard in the seat waved them through. Iris followed Alexander as he walked into a nearby elevator and hit a series of buttons, 4, 17, 6, 3. At that, there was a strange "chunk" sound and the elevator began descending below the ground floor. "So, Iris," he said. "Do you mind if we ditch the bike and get something better? I'm thinking a motorcycle."

"Not at all," said Iris. "I got it because it was quiet, within my means and had enough space to carry what I needed. Right now, it's just a means to an end." The elevator lurched to a stop and rolled the doors open. Inside was a dark room illuminated by countless computer monitors. Cables of all kinds were strewn everywhere and on various tables were beakers, dismantled electronic devices and other containers. Hunched over a monitor was a very tall man in a lab coat, around 200 centimeters, with a bald head and very defined facial features.

As he turned towards Iris, she saw that, on both of his temples was smeared a strange grey substance which formed hexagons across his skin. He slowly began walking towards the pair, mechanically raising one of his hands. "Alexander Chloraker. Greetings. I am not acquainted with your companion." Alexander turned to Iris and said "This is Fulgur. Just Fulgur. Don't mind him, he's a very friendly person once you get to know him, he's just dealing with a lot."

"Dealing with a lot?" asked Iris. "Yes," replied Fulgur. "Approximately 36% of my brain is entirely artificial and more is converted every single day. I am gradually losing the ability to express myself in human terms." She found this immensely creepy, but came to realize that anyone willing to deal with them in their situation must be at least a little unusual.

"Before anything else, I must make you acquainted with laboratory policy," he began. "There is to be no magic of any kind. Use it within the lab and you will be expelled with no further aid given. Do not touch anything without explicit permission. Do not take any photographs or recordings of the laboratory. Do you have any questions?"

"Yeah, why no magic?" asked Iris. "There are very sensitive experiments and equipment within the laboratory and, from experience, nearly all magi have the control and precision of a flamethrower," he explained. "That, and he doesn't want to leave traces to piss off the SCA," interjected Alexander. "Correct," said Fulgur. "It is not within my means to resist a government paramilitary and thus the optimal strategy is to avoid confrontation."

Iris thought it might have been better to avoid dealing with them entirely if that were the case, but she was smart enough to keep her mouth shut. Alexander, instead, spoke up. "I need a favor. Can you give her a hand?" At this point, she noticed that Fulgur spoke in a monotone and had absolutely no facial expressions. "What does she need aid with?" asked Fulgur.

Thinking it easier to just show it, Iris held up her right hand and gradually undid the bandages. Painful sterilizations had kept the stump from getting infected, but it was still far from a clean amputation. "I see. Your request was not an expression. Do you have any special requests for a new hand?" asked Fulgur. Iris thought it over.

Just what would she like her new hand to do? She had the opportunity for it to exceed her previous biological implement. "Will I be able to use magic through it?" asked Iris. "That is impossible," replied Fulgur. "There is currently no technology for producing artificial magic circuits. There is technology for producing Magi-Cores of various kinds, but that is expensive even beyond Alexander Chloraker's reach." Damn, so she would grow even weaker as a mage with every body part she replaced. She would just have to live with that.

"What about a shock function? Advanced sensitivity and precision? Data storage? Electric shock? Blade fingers?" Iris babbled on about potential abilities, as seen in various media she had consumed. Fulgur explained, "All of those are within acceptable parameters. However, it will take time to produce. Show me your remaining hand." Fulgur walked towards her and she held out her uninjured left hand. He roughly grabbed her and dragged her towards a device of some kind before setting it down on a table of some kind with a bar of light underneath.

"Hey, jeez!" Iris yelled. Unperturbed, he commanded her in his characteristic monotone, "Remain still for a few minutes. I will need this data to construct your new hand." The device whirred and shifted underneath her before several arms jutted out, passing lasers all over her remaining extremity. She spoke. "How long will my new hand take?" Fulgur replied, "Approximately a week. That is as quickly as it can be made."

"Well, damn." All things considered, Iris was privileged to be able to get a new hand, and that quickly, too. Many people who lost body parts weren't as lucky. "Know any good Life magi? Or can a new hand be cloned or something?" she asked. In truth, she was not very informed about cutting edge technology like this. She wasn't informed prosthetics like this even existed, so she wondered what else she was ignorant about. Alexander shook his head. "There are Life magi who are skilled enough to do such a thing, but accessing them is incredibly impractical, even for me. As for a clone, that's beyond Fulgur's abilities."

The idea of anything being beyond this strange man was astonishing to Iris. Eventually, the machine clicked and the arms retracted back into the bizarre table. Fulgur tapped at a nearby keyboard for a minute or two then turned to her. "Fabrication processes have been initiated. Return to this lab in one weeks time and I will attach your new hand." She stood up and turned back to Alexander. "Any plans for the next week?" she asked.

"Depends, really. What do you want to do?" said Alexander. Iris walked with him towards the elevator as she thought about it. She was now a fugitive hiding from a government paramilitary dedicated to suppressing and controlling the supernatural. For a young person with her entire life ahead of her, it's not a position she wanted to be in. She could flee to another country, but then what? They might have similar organizations, which would put her right back where she started. And though she was quite knowledgeable, she only knew Aenglic in the Gamman dialect, which would out her as a foreigner immediately.

"I think," Iris began, speaking slowly. "I think I want to fight. The cult which killed my father has been wiped out, so I can't take revenge. The SCA didn't do a damn thing to stop them." Alexander replied, "You sure? The SCA is a formidable opponent and there are things I won't be able to protect you from. If you want to destabilize them, you're going to face extremely dangerous opponents. There's no way around that. I'll teach you everything I know, but I can't guarantee it will be enough."

Alexander punched a few buttons on the elevator and it lurched upward. Iris continued, "I'm sure. It's what I want to do. Though having one hand makes things difficult." They stood in silence for a moment before she asked, "Who is this Fulgur guy, anyway? What the fuck's on his head?" He chuckled at her bluntness. "It's a long story. But basically, he's a very smart scientist who my father worked with, long ago. They've long since fallen out but I've kept in contact. As for his head, he shot himself one night when he found out his wife was cheating on him."

"He, uh, shot himself?" Iris was surprised anyone could still live and work after that. "Yeah," Alexander continued. "At the time, he was researching this bizarre clump of nanomachines we called the Grey Cloud. It somehow simultaneously existed as a solid, liquid and a gas. As he fell to the floor, he knocked the vial over and it rushed into his wound. It entered his body and reconstructed his brain. And he told you what the effects of that are."

Though Iris certainly wasn't very proud of where her decisions had led her, what Alexander said made her realize there's always someone who has it worse. "Fuck. And I take it part of his work is finding a way to reverse that?" she asked. Alexander replied, "Bingo. He still has emotions, but they're dulled. He wants to retain what he can and bring back what he has lost before he becomes more machine than man."

Eventually, they reached the ground floor and walked out of the building. Iris followed Alexander back to her bike and waited as he opened his prepaid phone and began a phone call. "Hey, Lewis? Yeah, can you bring a motorbike to the parking center near Ankas Drive?," he requested. "Yeah, high power, inconspicuous, with space for two. Middle floor, got it. I'll meet you there." After ending the call, he turned towards her and said, "Let's go. Time for an upgrade." She smiled, feeling good about being able to get something better than the electric bike they were using.

It only took a couple minutes for them to ride to the structure Alexander mentioned. They waited among many other cars until a middle-aged man pulled up in front of them on the motorbike he had requested. It was surprisingly quiet yet its sleek design concealed a great deal of power. The paint job was understated, leaving no shining parts. The bike's maneuverability left absolutely nothing to be desired, judging by the way Lewis deftly maneuvered it. He got off the bike and tossed the keys to Alexander, who easily caught them.

"Your bike, sir," said Lewis. "And if I might make a suggestion, don't let her drive it until you're sure she's ready. It has much more power than one might realize." Alexander smiled at his frank assessment. Iris was mildly irritated but remained silent. "Yeah, just one more thing," said Alexander. He turned to the electric bike they had ridden in on and put his hand on it. After a moment, it began to dissolve, cracking and breaking apart before laying as a pile of broken metal. That, too, soon dissolved, leaving only a pile of dust. "There. No evidence."

"Jeez," said Iris. "What was that?" Alexander replied, "Making sure it can't be tracked. Combining Shadow with Earth is very helpful." She was mystified by the concept. "You can combine elements?" asked Iris. "Of course you can. Shadow is very versatile. Combine it with Fire to burn mana itself. Combine it with Water to break it apart into useless molecules. Combine it with Earth - as you saw, to dissolve it and turn it to dust. And metal is Earth. Combine it with Wind and you can cut through magical constructs. Combine it with Life to create horrid mutations. Combine it with Death and you can eventually learn to shatter souls. Combining it with Light is theoretically impossible, though I'd love to see someone try. Combine it with Space and you horrifically warp and distort it. Combine it with Time and you create areas of irregularity, where different objects experience it at different speeds."

Iris realized she commanded an extremely dangerous power, and though Alexander was far more experienced with it, she had more natural ability. Her demonic ancestry would serve her well in the coming conflicts. "I take it the latter two aren't very practical," said Iris. "Of course," said Alexander. "Thanks for the ride, Lewis. You're free to go." As he walked off, Alexander put on a helmet and tossed Iris one, as well. Strangely, she felt a small pressure in the side of her forehead when she slipped it on.

Alexander mounted the bike and gestured for Iris to follow him. She did so, gripping around his waist once more. Rather than roaring to like, the bike gave a small sputter, which only caused Iris to be more surprised when it sped off towards the exit. "Whoa!" she yelled, gripping Alexander tightly. He deftly maneuvered it through the parking complex, out to the street and easily into the road. "How much fuckin' power does this thing have?!" she yelled. Alexander yelled back, "More than you think!" She wasn't one to keep up with motorbike technology, but she was still astonished at how something so quiet could be so fast.

With the powerful bike beneath them, it didn't take long for them to reach their hideout. Internally, Iris breathed a sigh of relief when she saw that it was untouched. Alexander had apparently also received the keys to the house from Lewis, as evidenced by how he casually unlocked them. "No more window climbing, huh?" said Iris. "Yup," replied Alexander. "I also have the keys for a few other houses."

They entered and locked the door behind them. Exhausted from the trip, Iris collapsed onto the floor in their bare living room. Alexander soon joined her, sitting against the wall. "Hey," she asked. "So is that Lewis guy your butler or something?" Alexander replied, "Yeah. Family servant. Knows better than to blab around about me, though."

"So, can you tell me about how the SCA is viewed among the rich?" asked Iris. Alexander thought for a bit, then said, "It really depends on the family. Some of them love the idea of restricting magic among themselves and outright fund the SCA for the opportunity to do that. Others want to be able to lord it over the working class and use it as a tool to solidify their own power." Iris replied, "That's fucking scary. My next question was going to be if we should work with your father against the SCA, but that's out of the question."

"Oh, yeah," said Alexander. "You do not want to get involved with him. He will use you for everything you're worth then discard you when you're all dried up." Merkuroth took the opportunity to speak up. "I would also advise against working with the upper classes. By their very nature, they exploit others and will have very little empathy for your situation. I am beginning to think Alexander is a very rare exception." Still, with so little support, that made their situation difficult. "That just leaves us with you, your resources and your friends, huh? Fuck," swore Iris.

"I'm making some freeze-dried mac and cheese," said Alexander as he stood up. "You want anything?" Iris looked up at him as he walked into the kitchen and said "Yeah, make me some, too." Their pizza was finished and the boxes discarded, leaving them hungry. Alexander, in particular, should be drained since he used magic. While he cooked, Iris grabbed her laptop and booted it up. It didn't take long for her to pirate a few movies she had wanted to watch, before it all happened. Soon after, he came in with two of their mess kits and around six packages worth of freeze-dried food.

"You wanna watch some movies?" asked Iris. "The Amazo locker doesn't have my deliveries yet so we have time to kill. And I can't really exercise, since, well." She held up her right arm. "Sure," replied Alexander. He sat next to her as she awkwardly started the movie, still not quite used to using a computer with one hand. A science fantasy epic about a young woman on the run started and they both stared at it quietly.

After around a half hour, Iris broke the silence. "This kinda sucks. It's way too self-inserty and the protagonist doesn't make smart decisions at all." Alexander replied, "Yeah, I agree. Not very fun." Iris leaned up against Alexander's shoulder and he glanced at her before wrapping his arm around her shoulders. She spoke again. "You know, I never met my mother. Turns out my father killed her."

"He did?" asked Alexander. "Yeah," said Iris. "Back in that interrogation room. They showed me a note from him. He left me a bunch of shit and a note about how he never wanted me to get involved with magic. And all things considered, I can see why. It sucks since he was such an amazing dad otherwise. You're warm," said Iris. "You're cold," said Alexander. "Really cold. Wait, I need you to try something." He removed his arm and turned to her. "Hold out your hand and try to move the water in your food."

"What?" said Iris. "Just do it," commanded Alexander. She did as she was told and focused intently on the food. After a bit, the liquid inside the mess kit began shifting around. "That's new," said Iris. "Care to explain?" Alexander was quick with answers. "You acquired the Water attribute. I have no idea how, given that you said you only had Shadow, but it's something new to train."

"And what does that have to do with me being cold?" asked Iris. Alexander explained once again. "Mutations accumulate as your skill and attunement to the attributes grows. With Fire, your body temperature rises, you gain red eyes and you become capable of seeing along the infrared spectrum. With Water, your body temperature lowers, you gain blue eyes and you see along the ultraviolet spectrum. With Earth, your bones and muscles become more dense. With Wind, your joints become hypermobile and your body loses mass. With Life, your blood becomes bright red, metabolic processes increase and you heal more quickly. With Death, you gain a pale complexion and eventually the ability to see spirits. With Light, you gain a faint halo. With Shadow, horns. With Space and Time, I'm not too sure about. My abilities with Space are very basic and I've never encountered anyone with Time."

"Wait." Iris felt her forehead and noticed a small lump on top. "I think you're right. Seems like a horn to me." In the glow of the laptop, Alexander looked at her. "Blue eyes, horn, low temperature, yeah. You're mutating." That simply left one mystery. What gave her these attunements? The two of them resumed watching the movie, her being uncomfortable with learning of the mutations but not able to do anything about them.

To her knowledge, she was born with Shadow. She never swam much, usually took quick showers and was rarely caught in thunderstorms. Her first contact with magic was finding her father sacrificed to summon Merkuroth. After that, she evaded the SCA, then went on an expedition to the demon cult's headquarters where she lost her hand and was captured. "Have you figured it out yet?" asked Merkuroth.

Damn demon probably knew already. Iris thought it all over, before remembering her fight with Francis. He had cloaked his blade in mystical energies before severing her hand. That was it! "I got it. It happened when I fought Francis, that SCA lieutenant. I got infected through his blade. Which should mean I also have his Wind and Life attributes." She would have chosen Fire and Earth if she were given the option, but she certainly did not want her magic circuits to explode.

"Using that was my backup plan for escape if Alexander hadn't managed to overload the collars," said Merkuroth. "Always keep hidden weapons and knowledge so that your enemy underestimates you."

Unable to hear Merkuroth, Alexander spoke. "That would explain it. I didn't know too much about Francis, as I had no prior contact with the SCA, but my father's documents on squads operating in this area indicated he was Water/Wind/Life/Light." Iris resumed leaning against him. She now had more abilities to develop and more opportunities to defend herself and strike at her enemies.

CHAPTER 10: ARKUROTH

"Pass me the scalpel, brother."

I stared down at the Arisen before me, the beastwoman I admired so much. She would be the prototype for a new form of people, a sapient capable of participating in a society-wide hivemind. Conflicts, misunderstandings, mercilessness - all of these would be eliminated. Everyone would be equal, and everyone would work together. To get to this point, many sacrifices must be made. I am well aware of that. And operating on the woman I admired so much would be part of that.

Arkuroth, my twin brother, handed me the scalpel. The Arisen was connected to many ancient medical devices - cardiograms, an infusion pump, an oxygen mask custom-designed for her lupine features. Of course, it was all redundant, only there in case my brother's focus on his magics should waver. He, after all, was maintaining her life functions, come what may. I held the scalpel in front of me before plunging it into my own chest. The pain was dull and distant, but I was fully aware of it. The scalpel easily sliced through my flesh, and I soon made further horizontal incisions on the top and bottom of that. Afterwards, I peeled back the skin flaps, exposing my ribcage and the organs behind it.

"Bonesaw, please." I set aside the scalpel and took the proffered tool. The worst part of sawing through my own rib cage was the noise. It was like a spongy form of wood and I felt the vibrations throughout my body. Eventually, I took hold of one rib and yanked it, listening to the cracking sound as it came out. Only 23 more to go.

Eventually, I had all of my ribs on the table beside me, prepared for future reattachment. My brother would be able to handle that more easily, without having to keep the Arisen's body functioning. I looked down at my still beating heart, my respirating lungs and beneath them, my liver. What I sought, however, were the thin, stringy objects nestled between my organs. "Another scalpel, brother." With that, I carefully and precisely reached into my chest cavity and sliced through one.

It was like a bolt of lightning throughout my body. A chill spread through me, something precious having been forever severed. My magic circuit was detached and the remnants of it would soon die and become useless. I knew that in doing this, my own power would be permanently reduced, my command over my magics lessened. But that was another necessary sacrifice for the new world I sought to build. Slicing through the other end was much easier, the circuit already non-functional.

Seven more. I knew that it wouldn't be pleasant to go through them, but eventually, I did. One at a time, I removed them and set them aside, knowing how precious they were to this operation. "Brother," I said, "My ribcage." He looked up from the Arisen woman and held out his hand toward me. One by one, I replaced my ribs and he fused them back on with his Geyarask magics. Afterwards, I slowly replaced the flesh flaps of skin and muscle and he similarly healed them. Once more, I was whole.

That simply left the Arisen. With new, cleaner tools, I cut into her flesh, opening another large flap of skin and muscle, before peeling it back. My brother's attention undivided, he was able to aid me by using his magics to crack the ribcage and allow me to detach the ribs more easily. I stared at her organs, devoid of the circuits I had intertwined in my body. The first one, I simply laid into her chest. My brother caused her body to extend fleshy tendrils, absorbing the circuit and sinking deeper into her body. In time, they would grow and give her some portion of the abilities I commanded.

One by one, I added the circuits, giving a piece of myself to her. It wasn't long before I had finished and together, we reattached her ribs and healed her flesh. No scars would mar her beautiful skin, but in the end, she would become like me. A corrupted dark magus. "I am sorry, Isabelle," I said. "But you shall be the very first. The prototype for a new kind of person, one who will never harm another simply for their own gain. One day, the time may come when my goals are achieved. Then and only then may you end my life."

Iris awoke with a start, thinking back to the gruesome magical surgery employed in her nightmare. She felt sick, so she rushed into the bathroom. The feeling of nausea passed as soon as it came, leaving her standing over an empty sink. "Oh god, that was fucking disgusting. What the ever-loving fuck? Was that one of your memories?"

After recounting the dream to Merkuroth, he confirmed her suspicions. "Yes," he said. "That was one of my memories. I told you that I wished to achieve a goal that required many sacrifices. Causing harm to someone I cared deeply for was one of them." The feeling of disgust towards the demon was becoming all too familiar to her. "Who was that woman?"

"An extremely intelligent biologist and enginseer," said Merkuroth. "An Arisen who had commanded an expedition against me during my early days with the Cult of Lisantr. She hired mercenaries to salvage an ancient weapon I was similarly sent to acquire. We fought, I killed one of her companions. She hated me ever since, though I watched her from the shadows. She was an exceptional woman, capable of great things. I knew that I would need to harden my heart no matter what came."

"My brother aided me in my operation purely out of interest to see if it was possible. He had no possible stake in her life, though I took pains to ensure he would do everything in his power to keep her alive. The surgery was merely the first step. I forced her to learn to use her new powers, to command them as I have. Her potential was one tenth of mine, but she used it ingeniously, creating spells which would achieve their effects through procedural generation rather than outright force."

"She became a very potent necromancer, reviving everyone she had thought died unfairly. With that, she founded the Empire of the Fallen, dedicated to changing the world to one in which all undead would be able to live out the lives stolen from them. I attempted to aid her, as her goals were similar to mine, but she rejected every diplomatic approach I made. Understandable, considering what I had done to her."

"You just ruin the life of everyone you're involved with, don't you?" said Iris. Merkuroth was silent for around a minute. "Yes. My judgment is in error. That is why I trust yours and seek solely to aid you." Her disgust at having the aid of someone like him was palpable, but she wouldn't have been able to survive without it. Without him, the SCA would have captured her and either drafted her or made her into an experiment long ago. Perhaps he wasn't the root of the problem.

Magic, itself, was a corrosive force. Everything she had learned, everything she had been exposed to showed how people used it solely to harm others. Controlling people, setting up shrines to their own arrogance, outright killing them. Perhaps that's what she should direct her efforts towards changing. The SCA was no solution, given that they simply sought to control magic to aid governmental forces. Could she see an alternative course of action?

Iris resolved to think about her plans later and walked into the living room. She found Alexander practicing martial arts. There wasn't a lot of room to maneuver, but he made it work. She stared on as he practiced short punches, deflections and the occasional grappling move against invisible opponents. After a while, she asked him what he could teach her. She wasn't going to be missing a hand for much longer, so she wanted to get a head start.

Alexander's reply was simply to teach her to breathe. She found it utterly mystifying, but obeyed as they sat facing each other. Deep inhalations and exhalations followed. After a couple minutes, Iris asked, "Is there a point to this?" He replied, "I was waiting for you to say that. Power in martial arts comes from the breath. Without air, even the strongest person is helpless. Thus, you must ensure you're capable of proper breathing no matter what circumstances you are placed in."

It took five minutes, then ten. Then Alexander spoke up. "Always remember your breath. If you forget to breathe when you exert yourself, you die. If your enemy catches you off guard and you forget to breathe, you die. Don't ever let that happen. Now, I'll be teaching you the Kwan Ji style. You simply don't have a lot of power in your body. You're a woman, you don't have as much muscle mass and bone density as a man." Iris wasn't exactly too happy about that fact, but he was right. But she had started engaging in physical training ever since the day she found her father.

Iris followed as Alexander showed her basic maneuvers. First was deflection, avoiding allowing an enemy to land strikes. Next was evasion, not being where your enemy was attacking. Finally there were basic attacks, aimed at pressure points, nerves and joints. What she could learn was limited, given her single hand, but she practiced as hard as she could. After an hour's time, both of them sat on the floor, caked in sweat.

"So, have any plans for today?" asked Iris. "Yes," replied Alexander. "There's a few people I want you to meet, later on. People who also hate the SCA for their own reasons and might be willing to work with you against it. We're also moving houses. Pack your things." She took the first shower and made herself a huge brunch, having skipped breakfast in order to train with him. He soon joined her and they ate together before beginning to arrange their possessions in their bags.

Alexander took out a multitool, expertly dismantled the rifle and put it into his bag. It was much more compact and portable when not battle ready. "What is that thing, anyway?" asked Iris. "I never really got a chance to ask that." Alexander replied, "Magekiller rifles. The SCA gives them standard issue to new recruits. They fire high velocity AP rounds fueled with mana rather than gunpowder, hence this." He tapped the device previously attached to the receiver. "Most magi have some form of countermeasure against firearms, but it's a good weapon to those who haven't mastered their own abilities."

So it seemed the SCA put a lot of thought into their arms and equipment. "And their squads? Do they all operate like Francis', some people with guns to one stronger magus?" Alexander replied once more, "Yes. Sharp thinking. The thinking is that stronger magi should take command over weaker ones and direct them as needed against any potential threats. It's somewhat like non-magical militaries in that respect."

"Why are the squads so small?" asked Iris. Alexander said, "The SCA is spread very thin. Resources, personnel and territories are all stretched to the breaking point. More and more magi keep being born and very few willingly join them. Those who are conscripted often seek to find their own way out, one way or another." That might make their goal easier. An overtaxed enemy was far, far more vulnerable than a well-prepared one.

With nothing remaining, the two of them grabbed their bags, locked up the house then mounted the motorbike. They wouldn't be returning here when the SCA was on their tail. Alexander turned the keys and the bike came to life, soon after speeding through the streets. They rode in silence, being tired from their training and not having much to say. Along the way, they dropped by the Amazo locker and retrieved what Iris had ordered.

Their new house was much like the old one, a shabby home in a district where most of the residents didn't own their houses. The perfect place for fugitives to hide. Given that they packed and lived light, it only took around an hour for them to get their bearings. Mylar blankets, folded clothes for pillows and freeze-dried meals prevented them from needing to go out. Rotating between houses was their way of avoiding the SCA.

"There's something I want to ask," said Iris. "Is there anything I can do? Ever since we met, you've been protecting me and keeping me from harm. But I feel so useless. I hate it." Alexander thought for a while. "What's your skill set? With one hand, what you can do is limited, but for a smart girl like you, I know you'll be able to figure something out." Iris usually found Alexander's complements flattering, but now they were just grating.

"I'm really good with computers. That's the most important part. I can pick locks. I'm a mage, though a very weak one. Uhh, electronics are great, too." A 15 year old hacker like Iris was brilliant in her own ways. "In fact, why don't I teach you to pick locks? And use a computer. That would be a really good place to start." Alexander agreed. On her laptop, she showed him such amazing concepts as using a word processor to write documents and compose encrypted e-mails to friends. Previously, all of these things were done by his servants.

"I'd like to practice magic, as well." In the backyard, they set up empty soda cans on discarded scrap wood. Iris held out her remaining hand and shot small pellets of ice at them. They were very weak and only managed to tip them over. "Shit," she swore, then switched to Wind magic. She achieved only slightly better results, being able to blow the cans over fairly easily.

As for Life, she achieved slightly better results. Iris could manipulate dead cockroaches with difficulty, and twist their flesh into strange shapes. It would clearly take a lot of time and practice to achieve anything resembling combat readiness, or even practical use, with these magics. Alexander did his best to help her, but with different magics, he could only speak of the basics of mixing mana with the attribute then running it through their magic circuits.

"There's something else I'd like to tell you about," said Alexander. "Attribute-less magic. By simply running mana through your magic circuits without attuning it to any attribute, you can achieve various effects. For instance, you can transfer mana to another, use telekinesis or enhance your own physical abilities."

"I take it there's a catch," said Iris. "Yes, yes there is," said Alexander. "It's extremely inefficient. Swallowing the worms made the first ability possible, though it was still barely enough to get us out. Telekinesis is often deployed in barriers to stop enemy gunfire. And physical enhancement is often neglected by magi. They seek to practice their magics above all else." That could be a potential source of strength, thought Iris. If she were forever destined to be a weak mage in all attributes save Shadow, she could enhance her body as much as possible to gain an unforeseen advantage against enemies.

"So let's try something. Make a barrier," said Alexander. At his instruction, Iris channeled mana with no attributes through her magic circuits. Eventually, she managed to produce a small barrier which blocked pebbles he threw at her. "Very good," he said. "Just try to stay behind cover. It probably won't block a bullet like it does a stone."

That night, when they were eating together, Iris asked Alexander "What made you realize your father's a bad person?" It was a simple question, but he still grimaced. "Are you aware of black lung?" he asked in return. "No, what is it?" said Iris. "It's a condition you get from inhaling too much coal dust. The Chloraker Mining Concern had a lot of employees who were afflicted with it. It causes difficulty breathing, suffocation and eventually death."

"Now, what truly disgusted me was this," said Alexander. "My father spent a lot of money lobbying the government to ensure he wouldn't have to pay benefits to workers who got the disease. He could have just spent less to give them a pension for what they got while laboring to make him money, but he thought that was a better idea. I talked to him about why, and he said he doesn't want his workers to expect handouts. He said that once you give the little people something, they just want more, more, more. He fucking said it was their fault for not saving up enough of their wages to take care of themselves. As though he paid them what they were worth in the first place."

"Wow," said Iris. "Your father's an asshole."

"Yeah, that's not even the worst thing he did. I truly believe he needs to learn compassion. I think I hate him. But I don't want him dead. Just humbled," said Alexander.

Iris sighed. "Maybe we can do something about that, later on. But now, the SCA is our primary concern. Is there anything we can do to hinder their operations?" she said. Alexander took out his phone and began dialing. "Yeah, there might be. There's something else you can do. We'll gather all the intel we have and you can devise a plan."

"Wait, I can? I don't exactly have much experience with this." Iris wasn't very confident with her skills against large organizations, given that her previous confrontations with them resulted in her losing a hand and becoming a fugitive. "Well, everyone has to start somewhere," said Alexander. "We don't have much of a choice but to learn as we go."

With that, Alexander called Lewis and had him come by to drop off binders full of intelligence on the SCA. It would take Iris days to go through it all, but they had time. Hiding out in the rental home, they sought to go out as little as possible in order to limit potential exposure to the SCA. In addition, they had the radio Alexander had stolen from Francis when they fought him. With that, they'd be able to listen in to their conversations.

Iris spent days collating all of the information - personnel, tactics, equipment, maneuvers. Everything the Chlorakers had gathered for their own potential confrontation. Most of her waking hours were spent either going through the intelligence or training her own abilities. Eventually, she became capable of firing ice chunks at high enough velocities to punch through soda cans, slice them with blades of wind, make living matter dance on her command and create a decent enough barrier to stop rocks thrown at her.

"I have extensive experience with raids on enemy organizations," said Merkuroth. "I may be able to help you." Knowing what he's said about his past, Iris certainly didn't doubt it. "The first and most important step in assaulting an enemy, be they a squad, an organization, a convoy or even a simple individual is to gather as much information as possible. Once you know their strengths and weaknesses, you'll be able to more effectively compensate for and exploit them, respectively."

"The second most important step is to actually implement strategies in order to do so, insofar as you can. You must also be aware of the resources available to you, and frankly, they are meagre." Iris couldn't contradict Merkuroth on that point. "You simply do not have the forces necessary to take on the SCA. However, Alexander may be able to procure enough for a guerrilla strike. You will need to talk to him about what he can make available to you." She noted that the demon seemed very confident in the idea of her being a tactical leader of some kind.

"The third step is to actually execute the strike. You need to ensure everything you need is available to you and ready to be used. And, if not, you need to be able to adapt to alternate strategies as needed. If all else fails, you need to be able to exfiltrate with your life. Resources are replaceable, but in your case, that is not." Iris wondered if there was a case where one's life was replaceable. Given what he said about that beastwoman becoming a necromancer, however, she supposed there was. "Do you understand so far?" Iris nodded, sliding a paper out of a binder and looking it over. "Good. Now, that looks intriguing. A prisoner transport in two week's time."

"Yeah," said Iris. "Alexander and I have firsthand experience of their standard procedure when it comes to processing inmates. They keep them for a while, sometimes try to recruit them, before moving them to larger facilities. Once there, they're either imprisoned until they agree to join or experimented upon to learn more about magic. Sometimes quite brutally. He's told me rumors of vivisection. It's not something I want to let them keep doing, but I can't just stop them right now."

"The prisoner transport seems a very potent beginning. You could use their own tactics against them. Rescue the prisoners and offer them a choice. Either they run into the wilderness and get hunted by the SCA or work with you and help to fight it. Either will benefit you. In the former case, they'll tie up their resources and in the latter, they'll help you to actively harm them." Cunning, but brutal strategies always were Merkuroth's forte. At this point, Alexander walked into the room and tossed another folder in front of Iris. "I got us some allies," he said.

"And I'm sure you're ready to tell me all about them," said Iris, annoyed that he just covered up a bunch of her carefully sorted documents. "Yes, yes I am. They're the Brotherhood of the Leaves. In the long term, they have very different goals and culture to us. They effectively want to destroy modern civilization and return us to a hunter-gatherer life." Given that she quite enjoyed computers, Iris certainly wasn't a fan of the idea. "Are those really the sort of people we should work with?" she asked.

"Yes," said Alexander. "Because in the short term, they have as much reason to hate the SCA as we do. You know those ecoterrorist strikes you hear about on the news, causing brownouts and goods shortages?" Iris nodded. "I always just thought it was crazy extremists in more rural, undeveloped areas," she said. "Nope. It's mainly them. They're inherently decentralized and cell-based which makes it difficult for them to be tracked down. And they're more an idea than a hierarchical organization, meaning, anyone can be part of them, really."

"I suppose that makes them very useful to us," said Iris. "Yes, yes it does. But I've made it very clear that we are not part of them, we just have a common goal. And they're willing to work with us if we provide the intelligence and fight alongside them. So, what do you have?"

Iris fiddled with sheets of paper and her laptop for a few minutes. "This. This is what I have." Alexander took a few minutes to go through everything she had collated and prepared. "This could work. I really like the plan, I'd like to adjust our placement here. Now that we have more allies, we can also use a diversionary attack here." He pointed at various places on the map she had prepared. "Yeah. I'll finalize everything," she said quietly. "But before we go any further, there's something I need to tell you."

Merkuroth spoke up. "Be very careful, Iris. You might lose everything you've done so far." Alexander looked quizzically at her. "What is it?"

"There's a demon inside me." said Iris.

"A, a what?" asked Alexander. "A demon," replied Iris. "I've told you about when I first encountered the SCA. My father was sacrificed to summon him. They fucked up the containment sigils and died. I was the nearest host. I was unfortunate enough to be the first one to discover it, and, due to my great potential in the Shadow attribute, powerful enough to host it." Demonstrating what she was speaking about, she held out her hand. Shadows coalesced into another strange bust, this one of a man with a hood over his head and a strange metal mask. Burns could be seen on the edges of his eye sockets through the lenses.

"Iris, I don't think you realize what you've gotten yourself into. Do you realize just how dangerous demons are?" asked Alexander. "I can't tell you how many times I nearly died because of my father's experiments!" Iris continued speaking. "Yes, yes I'm fully aware.

Even he has told me as much. His name is Merkuroth, and he had a mortal life in another world before this one. But his actions ended up getting him killed. His own great power is what allowed him to retain his soul and eventually be summoned here."

Alexander looked absolutely furious at the revelation. He stared at her before speaking again through gritted teeth. "You need to get rid of that thing. I can't ever trust a demon." Iris sighed. "I was afraid you would react like this." Alexander interrupted her. "Afraid? Afraid! Of course I'm fucking afraid! We're fighting one monster and you turn out to be host to another one!"

"Do you want to talk to him?" asked Iris. "No. Not ever. Demons will tell you the most insidious lies in order to achieve their own goals. You can never truly control them for they will always seek a way to subvert and devour you. You are perhaps the most dangerous person I've ever encountered because you host one and you THINK you're in control!" Alexander stomped out of the room, slamming the door behind him. Iris covered her face in her hand. "Fuck."

"I warned you this might happen," said Merkuroth. "This is why I believe our partnership should remain secret. In truth, his fears are well founded. Most demons are insidious monsters. I am an exception solely because I had a mortal life in which I learned my ideals could not be implemented by my own hand. That is why I trust you so much."

"Shut up," said Iris. She sat there in silence, thinking over what she could possibly do to repair their relationship. Something so trivial as a pizza or a small gift wouldn't do it. She couldn't simply accede to his wishes and get rid of Merkuroth. If she even could, doing so would leave her even more helpless against the SCA. In truth, she needed him. She hated to admit it, but she had only gotten this far with his help.

With nothing else to do, Iris began working on the assault plan. She had read books by guerrilla leaders before, so she simply tried to implement what she had learned. Evade and outmaneuver, hide yourselves among the civilian population. Steal enemy equipment and use it against them. Avoid them where they are strong, attack them where they are weak. Always dictate the terms of the engagement, do not allow them to be dictated for you. She followed these principles as best she could, and knowing she was up against a covert paramilitary gave her a few extra opportunities.

Namely, Iris knew they wouldn't be operating openly. They rarely expected an attack like this, so they would likely be disguised as members of the Keras Police Department. She knew that their numbers were low, so she might be able to have a numerical advantage. And she also knew that, should the attack be blamed on the Brotherhood of the Leaves, that would only further reduce their pursuit of her and Alexander.

The intelligence Alexander had given Iris had some nearby servers for the SCA. It took her a few days, but she eventually managed to break into one of them and look for some useful intelligence. Unfortunately, there wasn't much specifically on there - personnel rosters, payrolls, ranking structures. However, it did confirm their upcoming prison transfer, so being completely certain of it was helpful. Iris left a rootkit on the server in case it might be useful. The other servers she might eventually be able to break into, but she didn't have that sort of time.

Eventually, Iris saw a car pull up in front of the home they were staying in. She watched out the window, fearing the worst, but the back door opened and the familiar hunched figure of Fulgur emerged. He walked up to the door and rang the doorbell before being let in by Alexander. She overheard snippets of their conversation. "...hand is ready." "She's over there in the..." Afterwards, she heard him walk through the house and knock on her door.

Iris gladly opened it and said, "Hello, Fulgur!" She quite looked forward to regaining the functionality she had lost, given how difficult it was to use a laptop and collate intelligence with one non-dominant hand. "Greetings, Iris," he replied. She felt embarrassed at the state of her room, merely being a laptop, a bunch of documents and a mylar blanket on the floor, but he was perhaps the last person to care about the state of her lodgings.

"Come with me, Iris," said Fulgur. He turned around and walked towards the front of the house. Iris was reluctant to leave the home they had been hiding in, but Alexander trusted this man, and so she did, too. She saw him reading a book in his room as they left. He didn't say a word as they exited the house, reached the car and entered the back seat.

"Your lab?" asked the driver. She was a black woman in a chauffeur's uniform. "Affirmative," replied Fulgur. Together, they drove to the skyscraper he used and proceeded underground to the lab. Iris noted that it had been quite a while since she had done anything without Alexander. Maybe he'd feel better after some time apart. But then, she thought that two days ago.

They reached a table where surgical instruments were set down. Iris didn't exactly feel good about the scalpels, bonesaws and syringes, but she realized that a lot of work was involved in something like this. "Do you wish to be conscious or unconscious during the procedure?" asked Fulgur. That was an easy question. "Unconscious." Fulgur flipped a switch and an operating table rose up from the floor. She climbed onto it.

"Hold out your left arm, please." Iris did so and he sterilized the inside of her elbow before poking the vein with an IV drip. She grunted at the pain, still not enjoying it even after everything she had been through. "Iris, can you count to ten for me?" Gradually, she felt the drugs enter her system and a wave of tiredness encompassed her. "One, two, three, four, uh, five, six." Soon, she lost consciousness.

"Uuuuugh." Iris' vision was swimmy and her body was unresponsive. She tried to get up but her legs simply wouldn't work right.

With all her willpower, she looked down on her right arm and saw a mechanical hand attached to it. It was painted with the light color of her flesh but she would likely be wearing gloves whenever possible. "Oh, fuck yeah," she murmured. "Looks badass." She felt Fulgur pick her up and carry her to the elevator, then to the lobby and out of the building.

"Alexander, Alexander's fuckin' cool, you know that? He's like, this rich kid, but not. He knows what fuckin' assholes rich people are! But he's willing to fight against that! How fuckin' cool is that! And he likes movies! He's total fuckin' shit with computers, though!" Delirious, Iris continued rambling to Fulgur as he carried her into the same waiting car and buckled her in.

"And you know, that's not all. He just fuckin', he fuckin' saved my ass when I was in that prison! God, he's so cool." Fulgur entered the car on the other side and said, "Yes, I agree, he is quite an admirable person." Most of her other ramblings were considerably less intelligible, ranging from how awesome the Robusta programming language is, the development of new technologies in the food industry to how hard it was to learn to pick locks. After a while, the car pulled up in front of their house. Once more, Fulgur carried her to the front door and knocked on it.

Alexander opened the door. "Greetings, Alexander." said Fulgur. "You will need to take care of her for a few hours. I have included all relevant instructions in her pocket." Iris hadn't noticed him slip it in. He likely did so while she was unconscious. Reluctantly, he took her from the scientist and carried her in.

"Hey, badass, how ya doing!" Iris continued her ramblings. "You know, you're like, the first mage I met who wasn't a total asshole. Maybe we could do something together. Do some fuckin', combo magic or some shit. Like in a video game. We're party members! Party members who just keep on fighting with each other against impossible odds! I wonder if you have anyone else who could join us! Well, maybe not now, but, uh, once we win!" Some people reacted strangely to anesthetic drugs. In Iris' case, she became very talkative about her interests. Alexander walked to her room and set her down on her bedding.

He subsequently took the packet from her hoodie's pocket and looked it over. It included basic instructions like keeping the implant clean, taking antibiotics for a few days (helpfully included), avoiding EMPs and extra features like additional strength and sensitivity, electric shocks at will and a data drive that could be extended from the pinky finger. Alexander sighed, likely because Fulgur no longer owed him a favor and he'd have to pay him back in the future for anything expensive like this.

Gradually, Iris sobered up. It only took around two hours, thankfully, for all of the drugs to work their way through her system. "Fuck, I'm hungry. Let's eat." Alexander turned his back to her and walked away, saying "Get it yourself. Demonhost." Damn. She had forgotten how he was still angry at her for that. Slowly coming to her feet, she chased after him. "Please wait. Alexander, please. Will you just talk to him?"

Alexander sighed again. "You know what, fine. I want to hear what he could possibly have to say to justify this." So, he turned around and waited. Iris, as well, waited for the strange sensation of her demon taking control. In a few moments, he spoke using her body. "Hello, Alexander. I want to thank you for taking care of Iris in such difficult circumstances. I believe I should start with something you may find odd. My name is Merkuroth. Merkuroth Chloraker."

"Chloraker? Is this some kind of a joke?" asked Alexander. Merkuroth continued. "It is not. It is not a common name. I theorize there is some form of connection between our worlds, which, after my untimely demise, enabled my summoning here. Sadly, I have no evidence, save our last name." Iris found the words escaping her own lips absolutely astounding. He had never mentioned his last name before, but then, what occasion was there to mention it? "You took her body. I can't talk to you when you've exploited someone like that."

"Neither of you have the skill to allow me to move to another host, sentient or otherwise. If you wish, I can help you develop it." Alexander turned and began walking away. "No. I'll never work with a demon. I can't do this. I'll leave you money, the supplies and a list of safehouses, but I'm gone." He retreated into his room and shut the door. Merkuroth put his ear against it in order to listen in.

They heard him dialing a number on his prepaid phone. After a minute or so, Alexander began speaking. "Hello? Lewis, is that you? Wait, who is this? Shit. You want to speak to your brother? He's here with me? What are you talking about? How do you know that name? Who is this, again?" Iris felt her eyes widen. Merkuroth kicked in the door, snatched the phone and broke it over his mechanical hand knee.

"We need to go. NOW." said Merkuroth

"What the fuck are you doing?" yelled Alexander. Merkuroth replied, "Trying to save us both. I don't know how, but I believe you were speaking to my brother. And if he knows we're living here together, and he knows I'm using Iris as a host, he will come. He is not someone you have EVER fought before. We cannot win. If you don't want to die, we need to move." With that, Merkuroth left the room and Alexander followed. After rapidly gathering the documents, intelligence and the laptop, they ran to grab the keys to the motorbike.

"Wait, give me that." Alexander grabbed his own bag before following them out the door. Merkuroth mounted the back of the motorbike before tossing Alexander the keys. "Go. Now." He caught them and got on the front, starting the bike. Afterwards, he gunned it. As they turned the corner, they saw a figure standing there, phone in hand.

Francis Sullivan.

His head was dented and he was wearing casual clothes. A simple T-shirt and pants. He raised one hand, cloaked in yellow energy. Suddenly, both tires of the motorbike popped and it skidded out of control. Merkuroth jumped off of the bike, rolling to a stop. A few gashes and bruises were all the injuries he sustained, a testament to extensive combat training in his own world. Alexander, however, was not so lucky. He was left next to the bike with a leg bending in an odd direction. He screamed in pain, the bike laying nearby in the middle of the street.

"FUCK! AAAH!" Alexander continued screaming. Francis slowly walked towards Alexander, his hands enveloped in a purple glow. Merkuroth positioned himself between them. He was entirely unarmed, so they had to rely entirely on magic and martial arts. As such, he enveloped his natural hand in a smoky black aura.

"Arkuroth, listen to me." Merkuroth spoke quietly, his words accented by Alexander's cries of pain. "If you want to talk, you cannot harm Alexander. He is a friend, both to myself and to Iris Kriemhild. And if you want to have a conversation, you cannot begin it by killing a friend." Arkuroth, inhabiting Francis' body, laughed. "Hurt him? I was going to heal his leg! How can we talk when we have that dreadful screaming in the background?"

Merkuroth was silent for a moment, then he stood aside. Iris was incredibly terrified of this man who had so easily disabled their vehicle and whom even Merkuroth feared. But she knew it was best to trust his judgment. Arkuroth continued his slow walk towards Alexander before kneeling down and placing his hand on his leg. With a sickening crack and a strange twist, it moved back into place as though nothing had ever broken it.

"What the fuck? I thought you were going to kill me!" Alexander was incredibly rattled by his actions. Merkuroth continued watching as Arkuroth said, "It depends on how this goes. Can we go inside and have some tea?" Merkuroth shook his head. "No. We talk here. How did you come here? And more importantly, what do you want?"

"The answer to the first question is simple," said Arkuroth. "Join me, brother. I seek knowledge and power in this new world. I know you want the same. Given your goals in our own, I can help you achieve the same here."

"No," said Merkuroth. "I lost. My ideals ultimately had no place there." Alexander got to his feet, looking himself over for other wounds. He slowly backed away from Arkuroth. He, however, continued speaking. "Don't be a fool, brother. You know you're no match for me in this body. Limited as it is, I can still deploy many of my old magics. And what do you have? A 15 year old who barely knows what magic is. All you need to do is take her body for yourself. The young one has much potential, and you can develop it. Or I can find you another host."

"I refuse. Arkuroth, you have never sought anything but personal advancement. Your search for knowledge knows no limits and your lust for power is utterly ruthless. You will never be a reliable ally precisely because of that. You will sacrifice whatever is necessary to pursue your own goals. And I know from experience that such a path leads only to ruin. There is no end point. There is nothing that will stop you. Only endless suffering in your wake." While Merkuroth spoke, they saw Alexander quietly put his hands on the bike. His hands glowed green and the metal silently twisted and shaped itself into two rods.

"Merkuroth. Brother." Arkuroth extended his hands on either side before tapping his forehead. "I left this in the hope you would recognize that I'm trying to help you. If anything, I should thank Alexander for his help in freeing me. Francis has an exceptionally strong will and only with this brain damage have I been able to seize his body. I'm the only reason you haven't been caught so far. I've stymied the SCA's investigation at every turn. Do you really think Alexander's homes wouldn't be the first place they'd check? I've done so much for you, and I'm giving you the opportunity to join me. Please. As the only family we have." Alexander finished his creations, dual swords made from the wrecked bike. He began walking, then running towards Arkuroth's back.

Merkuroth, instead, cloaked her hand in the same smoky black aura. "Leave. Now." At that, Alexander swung both of his swords at Arkuroth. He, however, simply ducked down and to the right, tripping Alexander then driving an elbow into his stomach as he fell. He slammed into the ground, spitting up blood as Arkuroth insulted him. "And after I was kind enough to heal your leg, too!"

Eyes wide, Merkuroth charged forward, his only weapon the Shadow attribute in his natural hand. Arkuroth held out both of his own, an arc of lightning crackling between them. Merkuroth carefully tracked the arc before it shot towards them, catching it and nullifying it with his own heavy Shadow magics. Arkuroth was astonished, and that let Merkuroth get in close. He reached out with his artificial hand towards Arkuroth but found it batted aside as he moved in for a trip.

He barely managed to avoid the attack by stumbling backwards and landing on his ass. Arkuroth spoke once more. "Anti-magic. I underestimated her. I won't do so again." Alexander, for his part, stumbled to his feet, collected the damaged swords and ran towards Arkuroth once more. Merkuroth jumped back upwards, swearing to himself. "Shitshitshit! Alexander! Keep him occupied!" At this, Iris internally spoke to Merkuroth. "I have an idea. That dent on his head. Maybe it's what's preventing Francis from taking control."

"So you would bring him back?" muttered Merkuroth. "You got a better idea?" asked Iris. "No. No, I do not. Even so, I'm unsure my martial arts are enough to get in close. You will need to be the one to do it.." Still, he charged forward, hoping to work in concert with Alexander to get an opportunity to disable their opponent.

They were a flurry of motion, Arkuroth easily evading and out-maneuvering Alexander in spite of his being unarmed. Occasionally, he would duck under a sword, at other times blast it away with a strange green magic. It was as though he were a dancer in their macabre game of death.

Iris took control and reached out for Francis' head, but at the last moment, Arkuroth ducked and jabbed an elbow towards her solar plexus. She barely managed to block it by intercepting it with his artificial hand but could not take hold to deliver an electric shock. She then moved in using the Kwan Ji style's low guard stance, deflecting one of Arkuroth's fists with her artificial hand. Gracefully, she evaded another attack and managed to contact him with her natural hand. That was all it took for a spell to be cast. His skull slowly undented itself and he stepped back, gripping his head. "Aaagh! No, no!"

"Alexander, listen to me! We don't have long, we need to go! Now!" Still spitting up blood, Alexander nodded. They ran in a full sprint away from the street they had been living in, away from the home they had been using for the past few days. Eventually, Iris, owing to being less trained than him, ran out of breath and had to stop. "Fucking fuck!" she sputtered out. They needed to find an alternative.

Together, they looked around and eventually found it. A small car in a nearby driveway. They didn't have the time to pick the lock, so Iris simply punched the window open, reached through the shattered glass and unlocked the door. They piled in and he reached to the keyhole, forcibly activating it by simply turning it until it broke. "Do you know how to drive?" yelled Alexander. "No!" yelled back Iris as they pulled out of the driveway and down the street.

"Holy shit. I don't see him in the rear view," said Alexander. "Let's make sure of that," said Iris, taking out her phone and dialing 911. "Hello, police? I saw three guys fighting! It was like nothing I've ever seen before, they were transmuting shit and levitating it towards each other! They were using swords, too! Yeah, Irasi Drive! Fucking insane!" After hanging up, she broke the phone in two and dropped it out the window.

"There. That should get the KPD after them, and possibly the SCA. Best case scenario, Arkuroth gets contained by the SCA. Worst case scenario, he's delayed for a while," said Iris. "It's too bad we couldn't just kill him," said Alexander. "Now he's guaranteed to come after us."

"Killed him? Are you kidding me? We were lucky to SURVIVE! Merkuroth is freaking out right now!" The demon normally was one to keep his cool, so Iris knew if something was enough to upset him, it was extremely dangerous. "I'm going to keep driving for a few dozen miles and hope we've lost him," she said. "What about the sword, the gun, fuck, everything?" asked Alexander. "Consider it lost," said Iris. "We barely managed to escape." She took a few deep breaths, calming his nerves after the intense fight. "The SCA will be in chaos dealing with Arkuroth. It's the perfect time for the guerrilla strike we have planned."

End of Part One: Fugitive

Author's Notes:

Hello! I hope you enjoyed reading part one of my story.

This was primarily inspired by a lot of media I like, as well as old roleplay sessions. Both concepts and characters from them make their appearance here. In a sense, I'm drawing out of my life experience to make this. Even if I haven't done anything as crazy as share a body with a demon or use magic to engage in brutal street fights.

It took me a long while to really write something, but I'm finally back into my groove. I'll be keeping at it, so I hope you look forward to it!

Special thanks to all my friends who gave me these ideas and feedback on my early writing. This is just part one, there's tons of things ahead!

Drink water, exercise and take care of yourself. It's way more important than you think.

www.ingramcontent.com/pod-product-compliance
Lightning Source LLC
Chambersburg PA
CBHW051431150726
48000CB00005B/2059